I0747747

GOODNIGHT SUZY

A Collection of Short Stories
by HANS JOSEPH FELLMANN

A Russian Hill Press Book
United States • United Kingdom • Australia

R
H
P Russian Hill Press
The publisher is not responsible for websites or their content that are not owned by the publisher.

ISBN: 978-1-7378246-4-0 (softcover)
ISBN: 978-1-7378246-5-7 (eBook)

Library of Congress Control Number: 2022911409

Cover Design by Beau Berkley

For my father: my laughter, my reason, my rock.

CONTENTS

AUTHOR'S NOTE

Some of these stories are true. Others are bullshit.
Don't go nuts over it. Just enjoy the ride.

VIKI LAFLEUR

I had my first crush when I was five. Her name was Viki, and she sat next to me in kindergarten. She had hair the color of cherry juice. I liked to trace her profile, running my eyes from her mouth to her nose to her forehead then into all that cherry. She raised her chin when the teacher spoke. She knew all our class songs. The one she liked best was the "International Peace Song." She sang every bit, even the part where Peace was in foreign languages. I could never get that part right. I wanted to put my lips on hers so she could kiss me those strange words.

One day during song time, I tried to copy her. I was able to say *Paz,*[1] but other than that I was lost. I coughed out the words like hairballs. Viki looked at me and smiled.

"You want help?" she asked.

"Okay."

She scooted her chair next to mine and showed me her notebook. Peace was written in Spanish, French, Italian, German, and Swedish. She ran me through the list. It was tough at first, but I caught on. I was able to mouth a few of the words; they were clunky but formed. I put my hand on her knee. A bigger hand ripped it off.

"Get away from her, poo-face," a boy said.

I looked up and saw two black dots staring back at me. They were lodged in a face with orange freckles and a

---

[1] Peace. (Spanish)

knobby chin. The face belonged to a boy called Norman. He wasn't the most handsome, but what he lacked in looks, he made up for in meanness. He leaned in and put his arm around Viki. She shrugged and glanced at me sidelong. I wanted to grab my crayon and jab it in Norman's eye. The bell rang before I got the chance.

I was fuming when I got home for lunch. I stomped past the ham sandwich my mom had made and into the backyard. Our dog Tommy pranced up to me with a stick in his mouth. I kicked it from his jaws.

"Screw you," I said.

He whimpered and walked away. I sat in the garden dirt. The lilies were blooming. I stood and took a closer look. I rummaged around and found a lily I liked. I brushed the snails off the stalk and wrapped my hands around it. I leaned back and pulled. The lily popped from the soil with a rubbery sucking noise. I lifted it high. It was bruised and bent where I'd gripped it. Its spathe bore a tiny hole. But other than that, it was perfect. I smiled and took it inside. I riffled through my mom's stationary drawer and found a blue ribbon. I tied it gently around the lily's neck. I cut a paper square and taped it to the ribbon. I wrote a note with a Magic Marker.

to Viki. i lov u.

I put the lily in my backpack and brought it to class. I hummed as I walked through the door. Viki sat at her desk with her notebook open. I sat beside her.

"Hi," she said.

"Hey."

I took the lily from my backpack and gave it to her. She grinned.

"Thank you. Now, I have two flowers."

"Two?"

Norman walked out of the boy's room. His lips tightened into an asshole. He sat on Viki's other side. She held the cheap carnation he'd given her against her chest with my lily. She closed her eyes and rocked the flowers. Norman and I glared at each other over her nose. The air around us swelled and splintered. A nerve in my head burst.

"She's my girlfriend," I screamed.

"Nuh-uh. She's mine."

We went back and forth. Viki crinkled her brow.

"C'mon guys. Can't I have two boyfriends?"

The thought was unsettling. We found it in our hearts to compromise.

A month later she changed schools and left us both. Her memory slowly faded. To keep it from disappearing, I wrote a short story. It was about a knight who lived with his redheaded wife and daughter in a small village. Their lives were perfect except for one thing—the stupid dragon with the orange freckles who snuck into the village at night and ate people while they slept. The knight eventually slew the dragon and chopped off his head. He was hailed a hero, and he and his family lived happily ever after.

I saved the story in a special folder. The years rolled by. I grew older and taller and more angsty. I had a few crushes, even a girlfriend, but they went poof after high school. I was alone in junior college. I replaced women with angry music. One evening, I was storming around L-Town,[2] listening to Horrorcore.[3] As I made evil faces and spit flows, I crashed into someone.

"Dude, watch it," a voice said.

I looked up and saw my buddy, Mikey. His eyes were ringed with purple. He was massaging his shoulder.

"Shit man, you okay?" I asked.

---

[2] Livermore, California

[3] A subgenre of hip hop that draws inspiration from dark and often horror-themed content such as the occult, slasher films, mental illness, drug abuse, rape, and murder. Famous horrorcore artists include Tech N9ne, Insane Clown Posse, Geto Boys, and Brotha Lynch Hung, who has been described as the subgenre's creator, despite having stated that he is "more rip-gut cannibalism" rap, than horrorcore.

"Haha. Yeah. This ain't your doing."

"What happened?"

"I was partying all night at a strip club in the City.[4] I know the owner, so they let me in."

"Which place?"

"Pink Velvet. The girls there are fuckin' banging, especially this one chick that was dancing last night. She had long legs and crazy red hair. When I got a lappy from her, I realized she went to kindergarten with us."

"What was her name?"

"She said it was Candy, but I knew she was lying. I got her a drink and she told me."

"Was it Viki LaFleur?"

"How the fuck did you know?"

"Lucky guess."

"Bullshit. Tell me."

"She was my first crush."

"Haha. She was everybody's first crush."

"Yeah."

"You wanna see her again?"

"I'm not going to that strip club."

"No, she's a waitress at Cindi's."

"Seriously?"

"Yeah, I'm going there on Friday to get an application. You should meet me and say what's up to her."

"Okay."

Thursday night was torture. I knew Viki would look beautiful and that terrified me. Not that I was so bad-looking myself. But my hair was thinning and my wardrobe needed a serious update. I agonized over what to wear, finally settling on black jeans, a black and white plaid, and a black visor. I dressed and faced the mirror. I looked like a goth lumberjack with the top of his hat

---

[4] San Francisco

scissored off. I couldn't go to the diner like that. I needed something that would make Viki realize what a stunning specimen I was. I sat at my desk and thought. An idea came. I rifled through my drawers and found the short story I'd written. I stuffed it in my backpack and went to bed.

I drove to Cindi's after class, sweating the whole way. Mikey was outside smoking a cigarette.

"Why do you have your backpack on?" he asked.

"'Cuz I don't want someone to steal it."

"This ain't Detroit, bro."

"Whatever. Is Viki here?"

"Yeah, she's in the back getting changed. I told her I'd grab a table."

"Did you mention I was coming?"

"Nah man, I thought you could surprise her."

I took a deep breath and walked inside. Mikey snubbed his cigarette and followed me. We picked a table in back and ordered Cokes. I sucked mine down and ordered another. Mikey sipped his and squinted at me.

"When was the last time you got laid?" he asked.

"What?"

"You heard me."

"I don't know, a few months ago."

"My ass."

I ignored him and finished my Coke. I felt the urge to piss. I scooted from my seat. Mikey snapped his fingers.

"Oh, there you are," a woman said.

I crossed my legs and gripped my crotch. I heard the tock-tock-tock of high heels. The room suddenly smelled of hibiscus.

"Hey you," Viki said.

She leaned over and hugged Mikey. The zippers of her leather jacket ticked on the counter. Her hair shone like waves of rubies. She tossed it over her shoulder and stood back.

"Who's your friend?" she asked, clicking her nails.

"I don't know," Mikey said. "Who are you, friend?"

I raised my chin.

"Hey Viki. You remember me?"

She squinted. Something in her eyes softened.

"*Oh yeah*, you're that, uh, kid from kindergarten."

Blood rushed to my face. She reached in her purse and grabbed her keys.

"I'd love to stay and chat, but I have a second job. Anyways, it was crazy seeing you after all these years."

She waved and left. She crossed the lot and pressed her key fob. A shiny black Mustang beeped. She slipped inside it, revved the engine, and peeled out.

"I guess she's makin' good money shakin' that ass," Mikey said.

"Shut up, dude."

I spent the weekend in my room. The smell of eggs and chorizo brought me out. I found my folks in the kitchen. My mother was at the stove cooking breakfast, and my father was at the table reading the paper. I said hi and sat down. No one responded.

"Why are y'all so damn quiet?"

"You didn't hear what happened?" my mother asked.

"No. I've been asleep all weekend."

"There was an accident across town. Four people were killed."

"Jesus."

"A group of kids your age was out drinking at a bar that served them illegally," my father said. "They got in the car afterward and drove off. As they sped around the corner, the driver lost control and slammed into a phone pole."

My throat tightened. "Did the report mention any names?"

"Yes, but I didn't recognize any."

I grabbed the Alameda County[5] paper the next morning. Nothing about the accident was on the front page. I turned to the back. I found a photo of a mass of black metal crunched against a bent telephone pole. Glass and blood littered the street. An EMT was loading a sheeted body onto a stretcher. The headline read "Fatal Crash Kills Four in Livermore." I dug into the story for names. I recognized none. Then I saw "Viki LaFleur."

My stomach caved in. I ran to the bathroom and retched.

Back in the kitchen, my mother waited with knitted brow.

"Sweetie, did you know one of those kids who died?"

"Yes."

"Oh, I'm so sorry. Which one was it?"

"That Viki girl."

"Viki?"

She grabbed the paper. She scanned the article and pointed.

"Little Viki isn't dead."

"Huh?"

"She was drunk and beat up, but she survived the crash."

"How?"

"It says she was the only one wearing a seatbelt."

A month later, I found another article: "Drunk Driver gets 6 Years for Manslaughter." A photo of Viki was underneath. She was at the stand, giving her statement from a wheelchair. Her clothes were pressed and muted. Her face was red and broken. It looked like she was crying her hair through her eyes. I buried my face and cried with her.

---

[5] County in the San Francisco Bay Area, occupying much of the East Bay region. The population was 1,682,353 (2020), making it the 7th-most populous county in the state and the 21st most populous in the US.

PAYDAY

My mother parked at Nifty's and grabbed a cart. We went inside and shopped for dinner. I was especially helpful; I'd been promised a treat at the end. We filled the cart and went to the checkout line. A wall of candy was on our right. My mother told me to pick something. I rubbed my hands together and searched. The top rows were chocolate. The bottom rows were gummies and mints. I consulted the area in-between. I spotted something that wasn't quite candy but wasn't quite snack food. It was called a Payday. It had peanuts and caramel and nougat. Its wrapper was white, instead of black or brown. Its lettering was bright red, with blue outlining. I told my mother I wanted it. She placed it on the belt.

We paid and left. I helped my mother unload the groceries, and she gave me my Payday. I took it to my room and unwrapped it. It glimmered on my palm like a bar of gold. The corners of my mouth beaded with drool. I spread my lips and bit. The taste was sublime: a symphony of sweet saltiness underscored with notes of bitterness. I chewed with my eyes closed. A peanut dislodged one of my canines. Blood pooled in the crib of my jaw. I dropped the bar and ran to the bathroom. I put my face to the mirror and opened my mouth. My canine was crooked and bleeding like a tiny oil rig. I wiggled it with my tongue. A root of pain lit my jowl. I screamed with all my lungpower. My mother rushed into the bathroom.

"What's the matter, sweetie?"

I showed her my bleeding tooth.

"Awww, it's okay."

"No, it's not. It hurts."

"I know, honey, but this is normal. Everyone loses their teeth."

"Really?"

"Yes. And if you're a good boy and stop crying, I'll tell you a little secret."

"Okay, what?"

"Well, if you stick your tooth under your pillow, the Tooth Fairy will take it while you sleep and leave you some money."

I slanted an eyebrow.

"The Tooth Fairy?"

"Yes, the Tooth Fairy."

I considered Christmas and Easter. The logic was sound. I yanked my tooth out and stuck it under my pillow. I drifted off thinking about money. The next morning, I lifted my pillow. A ten-dollar bill was underneath.

"Holy crap."

I snatched it and ran to the kitchen. My mother was frying eggs. I held up my prize.

"The Tooth Fairy came," I exclaimed.

My father folded down the corner of his newspaper. "She sure as hell did," he said.

My mother sneered at him. She smiled kindly at me.

"Now you can buy your little Payday bars with your own money."

I hugged and thanked her. At the store with her later, I was an exceedingly good boy. I helped her pick out the groceries and even put them in the cart. At the checkout line, I saw my Paydays on the middle shelf. They were fifty cents a pop. I grabbed twenty.

"Oh no," my mom said. "You can only buy one at a time."

I balled my fists.

"What's the point of having my own money if I can't buy what I want?"

"You can buy what you want. But if you eat that many Paydays at once, your teeth will rot."

"So what? You said they're gonna fall out anyways."

"Suit yourself."

I bought my twenty Paydays. I carried them in a bag with both arms like a proud father carrying his newborn. I got home and went straight to my room. I piled the bars on my bed and dove in. I rolled around like a hog in shit. I smelled the peanuts, caramel, and nougat through the wrappers. I grabbed one and ripped it open. I bit it clean in half. I swallowed it and scarfed the other half. I chomped through ten more bars. My stomach hurt. Some whole milk took care of that. I repeated the process. I ate all twenty bars in two days.

On day three, I got shifty. I was craving a Payday bad. I explained this to my mother. She dropped the plate she was scrubbing.

"You ate all twenty bars?"

I looked down and kicked the hardwood.

"Kind of."

"Kind of? I can't believe you're not sick to death."

"Well, I'm not, so can you buy me some more?"

"Absolutely not. In fact, you won't be getting any more for a month."

I wanted to grab her by the ankles and flip her into the scalding dishwater. I knew my little arms wouldn't let me; I laced them across my chest and stomped off. I brooded in my room all day.

A week later, I was jonesing for a Payday. I had just seen a commercial where two big hands slowly pulled one apart, letting strings of caramel connect the peanutty halves. I ransacked my room for change. I found two arcade tokens and a dime. I threw them down and cursed. My lip hit the gap in my teeth. I skewered the hole with my tongue. I remembered the ten bucks from the Tooth Fairy.

I ran to the bathroom mirror and flashed my teeth. I wiggled them one by one with my thumb and index finger. I did the top row, then the bottom. Not a single tooth was loose. I looked at my missing canine. I figured its brother could go, too. I rummaged through the side drawer. I found scissors, tweezers, and a bag of beaded hair ties called Beanies. I knew scissors would be too painful. And the tweezers were too small. This left the Beanies. I fished one out and had a look. Its chords were stretchy and its beads were big. The metal piece in the center would balance the pull. I curled my upper lip and slipped the beanie around my remaining top canine. I made sure the metal piece was on the back of my tooth. I gripped the beads and inhaled.

Here goes nuthin'.

I jerked my arms forward. My tooth unrooted from my jaw like a baby tree stump. It spiraled downward and clinked into the bowl. A braid of blood followed it. I hocked my mouth empty and checked the mirror. There were slots where my canines used to be. I smiled devilishly. I plucked my tooth from the sink and washed my face.

That night, I told my mom about my tooth. She seemed incredulous that I'd lost it. She told me to put it under my pillow anyhow. I did so and went to sleep. I woke up in the morning and threw back my pillow. My face fell.

"One dollar?" I screamed.

I grabbed it and marched into the kitchen. My mother was at the stove, flipping pancakes. I lifted the crumpled bill.

"What's this?" I demanded.

She glanced down.

"Oh look, the Tooth Fairy came again."

"Did she forget her purse or something? This is one buck. Where's the other nine?"

"Didn't I tell you?"

"Tell me what?"

"For your first tooth, she brings you ten dollars. But for every tooth after that, she brings you one."

"Why?"

"Because the Tooth Fairy has bills to pay. And it's not like she can do much with your damn teeth anyway."

"Then why does she take them in the first place?"

She speared her eyes at me. I'd stepped into raw territory. I knew, like with Santa and the Bunny, that it was best not to unravel the mystery. I turned and left.

I went to Nifty's with her the next day. I helped with the shopping and bought my two Paydays. Back home, I took them to my room and devoured them. I still wanted more. I thought of ripping out another tooth. I knew the Tooth Fairy might get suspicious. The risk was worth it. I went to the bathroom and grabbed a Beanie. I wrapped it neatly around my bottom left canine. My mother opened the door.

"What in God's name are you doing?" she cried.

I shimmied the Beanie up and down like a little towel.

"I couldn't find the dental floss," I said.

She opened the cabinet and grabbed the floss. She slammed it on the counter and stormed off. I knew my Beanie scheme was through. I had to think of another angle.

I was in a stupor at school the next day. I stared at the blackboard throughout class. I walked to the playground at recess. I sat on the bumblebee slide and thought. I considered doing a face-plant off the top. I dismissed the idea as I didn't want to break my neck. I entertained taking a rock to my teeth, but I knew that would probably shatter them. There was a scuffle going on near the swings. Josh Hargrove was strangling this kid named Patterson for his lunch money. Patterson was a pathetic dweeb with a blond bowl cut and glasses that swallowed his face. Josh was tall and strong with creek-water eyes and a lizard's smile.

I stepped in. "Why don't you pick on someone a little bigger than Patterson."

Josh crumpled the money into his pocket. He looked at me and grinned. His teeth glittered like snake scales.

"Like who?" he said. "You?"

I wanted to run and hide. Instead, I made a fist. I leaned in and smacked him. My fist bounced meekly off his tit. He chuckled and lined up his stance. He drew his arm back like a harpoon and fired.

I remember spinning backward. I woke up facedown. I had a mouth full of blood and gravel. I spit it out and licked along my gums. My four top fronts were missing. The children around me cringed. I reached out and grabbed my teeth. I stood and faced Josh. I shook my teeth and stuffed them in my pocket.

"Lanks," I said.

"Anytime, shitface."

Josh punched out my bottom fronts and canines the next day. I hid this from my folks by wearing a ball cap real low and taking meals in my room. My mom got suspicious. On our drive home one afternoon, she asked me what was up. I smiled at her in response.

"Sweet Jesus!" she cried.

She almost lost control of the van. She screeched to the side of the road and stopped. She caught her breath and looked at me again. Tears quivered around her eyes.

"Who did this to you?" she said.

I removed my ball cap.

"Lo lun," I said.

"Then what in God's name happened?"

"Ly lell lau la lumblelee lide lan' las lembal'assed loo lell loo."

"Why would you be embarrassed about falling off the bumblebee slide?"

"Leeluz, Ly loo' li' lun'a lowz lums lat la LART lation."

"You do not look like one of those bums at the BART[6] station."

"Le Ly loo."

"Awww, c'mere."

She gave me a long, soft hug. We pulled apart and she smiled. I reached into my pocket and removed my fist.

"Loul ly lut leez luner ly lillow?" I said, opening my hand.

She closed my hand with hers.

"Of course, you can."

That night, I was manic. I had ten teeth, which meant at least ten more bucks. I put them under my pillow and tried to sleep. But all I could think about were Paydays, Paydays, Paydays. The peanut-studded bars swarmed my brain like giant bees. They broke apart in long strings of caramel, then slid down my gullet. It was a wonderfully torturous night. I ended it by guzzling a pint of warm milk. I woke up groggy in the morning. I lifted my pillow and rubbed my eyes.

"Li'ly lollars," I cried.

I grabbed the money and ran to the kitchen. My mother was serving my father breakfast. I held up the fifty-dollar bill with both hands.

"Loo' lu la Loo Larry lay lee."

My mother smiled. My father dangled his fork.

---

[6] Bay Area Rapid Transit (BART) is a public rail transportation system in the San Francisco Bay Area. It serves 50 stations along six routes on 131 miles (211 kilometers) of rapid transit lines.

"You better not blow that dough on those fuckin' candy bars," he said.

"Gerald," my mother spat.

He snorted and ate his scrambled eggs. My mother made me a fruit smoothie and took me to school. I was in outer space the whole day. I ignored my teachers.

My mother picked me up and we went to the grocery store. I helped her with everything. We put the bags in the van. I clicked my tongue.

"What is it?" she asked.

I raised a finger and opened the door. I ran into the store and got what I needed. The checkout lady gave me an odd look. I paid her and took my bag into the bathroom. I did my thing and went to the car.

"What'd you buy?" my mother asked.

I showed her a gigantic box of Band-Aids. I pointed to my mouth and frowned.

"Oh, you sweet boy."

We drove home and I went straight to my room. I wedged a chair under the doorknob and sat on my bed. I lifted the box of Band-Aids and tilted it forward. Payday after Payday tumbled out. They formed a pile the size of an ant mound. It was red, white, blue, and shiny. I plucked a bar from the top. I unwrapped it and held it to my nose. The smell of peanuts and caramel went up my nostrils like crack smoke. I opened my mouth and inserted the bar. I flitted my eyes and clamped my jaws. I waited for that gorgeous flavor. It didn't come. I pulled out the bar and looked. It was completely intact. I bit it again. My teeth snapped around it perfectly.

"Lesus Lice," I screamed.

I jammed the bar between my molars. I chomped off a few peanuts and chewed. They stabbed my tender gums. My mouth filled with blood. I dropped the bar and frowned. I looked at my cache of Paydays; they no longer glistened. I placed them back in the box one by one like little corpses.

GOODNIGHT SUZY

My grandfather gave me my first air rifle when I turned twelve. It had a long, black barrel and mahogany stock. A scope with perfect crosshairs was mounted on top. He taught me how to use it. I practiced in his backyard with old pill bottles. I lined them across a board over the drainage ditch. I tweaked the scope and fired. I hit two out of three bottles. He put his hand on my shoulder and smiled.

"Eso mijo. Así se lo hace," he said. That's it, son. That's how it's done.

Within six months, I was a little badass. I could place ten bottles in a row and crack 'em off the board. This got easy, so I put 'em around the yard—one in the fig tree, one in the lime tree, one in the fence hole, one in the ivy. I loaded four pellets and twisted my scope. Boom. Boom. Boom. Boom. Adios, muthafuckaz.

One time, I pulled some major James Bond shit; I hit a dozen bottles from various branches and bushes. My gramps came out in a flurry.

"Ya 'stás chingón, eh." You fuckin' killin' it, yo.

I stuck my gun butt to the ground and leaned cross-legged with my elbow over the barrel tip.

"¿Y?" I said.

He stood back and scowled. He told me a real marksman always rolled with modesty. I raised my rifle and popped off a round. A pill bottle across the yard jumped.

"How's that?" I said.

He stopped congratulating me. In my mind, I no longer needed him to. I had already mastered everything he could teach me. Accepting any praise from him seemed silly. I blazed my own little marksman trail. I shot all sorts of things, big and small. I had a special fondness for bottle caps. I liked blowing them off plastic bottles, so there was no sharp mess to clean.

One day, I found an expired two-liter of Coke in my grandparents' fridge. I took it and placed it at the far corner of the backyard hill. I went to my post and lifted my rifle. I looked through the scope.

Bring the bottle closer, a voice said.

I hunched my shoulder and scraped the voice from my ear. I repositioned myself and closed one eye. The cross-hairs touched the red cap.

Closer, the voice shrieked.

My nerves tingled. A set of long nails wrapped around my scalp. I stood and walked toward the bottle. I grabbed it, placed it on the nearby picnic table, and sat at my post. The tingling intensified. I breathed heavily and sweated. I raised my rifle and aimed at the cap.

Aim lower, the voice demanded.

"Why?" I muttered.

An invisible hand pushed down the barrel till it was pointed at the belly of the bottle.

Shoot, the voice whispered.

I pulled the trigger. A pellet ripped through the bottle. Cola glugged from both holes. It sounded like a gasping animal. I watched the brown liquid spill over the table. My crotch slowly tightened. I looked down and saw I had an erection. I dropped my rifle, ran to the bathroom, and slammed the door.

I didn't go near my rifle for weeks. It sat in the corner of my room like a haunted sword. I piled clothes and boxes around it. I forced it from my mind. One day, my mother came home from shopping with a huge smile on her face.

"Look what I got," she said.

She reached into her bag and pulled out a glass cylinder. It had a red base and a handled top.

"What is it?" I asked.

"A hummingbird feeder. Your grandma's been wanting one for a long time. I thought we'd go over there later today and surprise her."

My palms started sweating.

"Sounds good."

We drove to my grandparents' shambly house. We parked in their concave driveway and got out. They were at the door, smiling. We hugged them and my mother pulled out the birdfeeder.

"Oh, who's that for?" my grandma asked.

My mother frowned playfully.

"You know who it's for."

My mother put the birdfeeder out back. My grandma made enchiladas. We sat down and ate. Afterward, my gramps retired to the living room and my mom and granny went upstairs. I was alone at the table. I took the keys from my mother's purse and went to the van. I unlocked the back and opened it. I reached in and grabbed my rifle. My chest was burning. I went to the backyard and sat at my post. The birdfeeder hung from a tree branch, thirty feet away. I watched it glint and sway. Hummingbirds soon buzzed around it. I loaded my rifle and cocked it. I eyed the scope and fired. A single hummingbird fell from the air. The others shot off like darts. My stomach was sick with pleasure. I walked to the fallen hummingbird and lifted it by the wing. It dangled from my fingers like a lizard tear. A drop of blood ran down its wing. It reached the tip and swelled.

A hunger grew inside me. I killed more birds to feed it. They were a bigger challenge than my former targets—I had to wait for them to land and ready my weapon in silence. Even this didn't guarantee a kill. An unforeseen element, such as a cat or a strong wind, could send the birds flapping. I had many spots at my grandparents' for picking them off. My favorite was a neighbor's date palm. The birds swooped down and landed on the fronds. I waited for them to get comfortable, then I fired. I stopped their little hearts with one shot. They fell like the dates.

One afternoon, a swallow flew down and landed on a frond. I fired, and it bounced from the tree to the fence to the lawn. I walked over and found it in a little ball—a red hole in its wing. The bird jittered and blinked its black eyes at me. I lifted my rifle and placed the mouth of the barrel over its beak. My spirit filled with greenness. Those long nails coiled around my scalp. I laid my finger on the trigger. The screen door ripped open. I looked over and saw my grandfather. His cheeks were crimson with anger.

"*A los pájaros, no,*" he barked. Not at the birds.

My face fell into open-mouth violence. I looked back at the bird and fired. Its head splattered against the concrete. I thinned my eyes and chuckled. My grandfather came and grabbed the rifle. His head and hands were shaking. I looked into his eyes and saw a strange softness; it washed along my heart. My guts shrieked and curled. I let go of the rifle and ran inside. My gramps didn't rat me out. He even gave back my rifle. His only condition was that I never bring it to his house. I agreed.

I killed less after that—my backyard had bigger and bushier trees. They were harder to spot birds in. And their needles and branches were a bitch to aim through. One morning, I got an idea. I slung my rifle over my shoulder and climbed halfway up a tree. I waited a few minutes. The birds trickled in. They were the smaller kinds—swallows, sparrows, starlings. I'd capped dozens of these. They failed to pique my interest anymore.

An hour passed. A bird flew down and landed on the branch in front of me. It was a hefty pigeon with ashen feathers. The purple around its neck shone in the sun. I looked through the scope. The crosshairs dotted its wing. A smile widened under my ears. I gave it teeth and fired. The pellet snapped against the pigeon. It purred and fluttered and spiraled to the ground. I scrambled from my tree post. My heart was thumping against my brain. I ran up and took aim. The pigeon was dragging its wing over the grass. I waited for the sickness to will my finger. I saw my grandpa's eyes. They stared like two sad flames. I tried to cringe them from my head. They grew bigger and brighter and sadder. Soon they engulfed me. I dropped my rifle and squatted. My heart pulled open like a hot cookie. The tears came and came. The pigeon waited silently.

I stopped crying and went to her. I cradled her breast and lifted her. I took her to the garage and looked for something to put her in. I found an old shoebox. I placed her inside and upturned my hands. Her blood spotted my palms. I went in the house and grabbed the first aid kit. I came back and dressed her wound. I placed a handful of shelled sunflower seeds and a saucer of water in her box. I didn't know what else to do. I wanted her to live more than anything. I thought on her name. She looked like a Suzy. I told her everything would be okay.

By nightfall, Suzy seemed better. She was picking at her seeds and drinking her water. She was even walking a little. That made me smile. I reached out and ran my fingers along her feathers. She puffed up and pulled her head in. I took this as a sign she was ready for bed.

"Goodnight, Suzy," I said.

I placed the lid over her box to protect her from the bugs. I even moved her near the water heater so she'd stay warm. I clicked off the lights and closed the door. I went to my room. I stripped down and climbed under my blanket. Sleep came like a slow fog.

I woke up late the next morning. My head and heart were still. I dressed and went to the garage. I found Suzy's box where I'd left it. I reached down and removed the lid. Suzy was lying on her side. Her body was swarming with ants. I fanned them away and lifted her gently. Her feathers were cold to the touch. Her head hung to one side, and her eyes were shut peacefully. I took her to the backyard and grabbed a shovel. I picked a spot under the pine tree I'd shot her from and dug. I felt an emptiness in my chest— like something ancient had packed up and left. I laid Suzy at the bottom of the hole. I said a few words and covered her with dirt. I placed a stone above her grave. I sat next to it and stared off. The sun was blazing over the rooftops. It burned through my skin.

THE FIRST OF MANY

I woke up in the afternoon. A neighbor's lawnmower grumbled. I sandwiched my ears with my Freddy Krueger[7] pillow. Someone knocked on my door.

"Sweetie, Hawk is on the phone," my mother said.

---

[7] The fictional main character and villain in the *A Nightmare on Elm Street* film series. In life, Freddy was a serial child murderer who was torched in a boiler room explosion created by the parents of his victims. At the point of death, three serpent-like entities or "Dream Demons" imbued him with the power to enter people's dreams and torment, harm, or kill them—whatever he did to them in the dream world would manifest itself in real life. Freddy used this power to exact his revenge on the still-surviving children of the parents who burned him alive. He wore a dusty, brown fedora, a ratty, green-and-red striped sweater, and a bladed glove.

Director Wes Craven found inspiration for Freddy's character from several sources. The name "Fred Krueger" was the name of an actual kid who used to bully Craven in grade school. The malicious smile and dusty fedora, Craven took from a creepy old man who was staring at him through his bedroom window one night when he was a child. The green-and-red sweater he concocted after reading in *Scientific Magazine* that the pairing of these colors is extremely difficult for the human brain to process, thus making it disturbing for the viewer. The idea for the bladed glove came to Craven when he was pondering what the earliest weapon mankind might have feared was; he decided it was a predator's claw—the basis for the glove. The burnt skin was the result of Craven having seen a burn victim at a young age and being traumatized by the experience. Finally, the power to kill people in life by killing them in their dreams, was "dreamt up" by Craven after he read an article in the *L.A. Times* about a child refugee, who—after escaping the Cambodian genocide—refused to sleep because he thought he'd be attacked in his dreams and never wake up. "When he finally fell asleep, his parents thought this crisis was over," Craven recounted in an interview. "Then they heard screams in the middle of the night. By the time they got to him, he was dead. He died in the

I flung my pillow across the room.

"Shit, Mom. I'm sleeping."

She opened the door and handed me the phone.

"I'm *waaaay* too nice to you," she said.

I grunted and sat up. My mother shut the door. I put the phone to my ear.

"Yeah?"

"Dude, you're spending the night at my house," Hawk said.

"Am I?"

"Yes. I've got a plan."

"Great."

Twenty minutes later the doorbell rang. It was Hawk wearing a flattop, baggy jeans, and a faux leather jacket. A pair of black shades was wrapped around his snowy face. He straddled his Schwinn[8] and flexed his pecs.

"OK, Arnold,"[9] I said.

He socked me in the shoulder. I nearly fell on my ass.

"Thanks, fucker."

---

middle of a nightmare."

This story wasn't an isolated incident: dozens of Southeast Asian refugees in America, particularly young men in their 20s and 30s from the Hmong ethnic group, died for unknown reasons in their sleep during the 1980s. Some attributed this to the trauma they faced during forced migration. Others attributed it to chemical nerve agents the refugees may have encountered. The Hmong themselves believed they were being punished by the spirits of their ancestors for fleeing their homeland. Whatever the cause, the fatal ailment was later classified as Sudden Unexplained Nocturnal Death Syndrome (SUNDS). It has been investigated by the Center for Disease Control at length; however, the wave of SUNDS deaths among Southeast Asians, particularly the Hmong, in the 1980s is still unexplained.

[8] Schwinn is a bicycle company founded by German-born mechanical engineer Ignaz Schwinn (1860–1948) in Chicago in 1895. It became the lead manufacturer of American bicycles through most of the 20th century. However, it declared bankruptcy in 1992, and has since been a sub-brand of Pacific Cycle.

[9] Arnold Schwarzenegger. Austrian-American film actor born July 30, 1947. Former governor of California (2003 – 2011). He has starred in many hit films such as *Terminator I* and *Terminator II*, in which his signature look included a flattop, black shades, and a leather jacket.

"Watch your damn mouth, Johann," my dad yelled from the window. "And be home tomorrow at ten sharp. It's your grandmother's birthday."

"Yeah, yeah."

I went to the garage and grabbed my bike. Hawk and I peddled off.

"So, what's this big plan of yours?" I asked him.

"We're gonna hit Larry's."

"Larry's? We always pilf bargs[10] from that old fart. How is that new?"

"'Cuz this time we're gonna jack *snalk*."[11]

I asked him how we'd manage that. He pointed to his baggy jeans.

"These have extra deep pockets. Just got 'em at the mall."

We rode to Larry's and dropped our bikes. Hawk pushed the door open, and I followed.

"I hope you know what you're doing," I whispered.

Larry was behind the counter watching TV and scratching his belly. I approached him and fiddled with the candy. He turned and glared at me through his thick specs. I held up a bar and smiled.

"How much for a Payday?" I asked.

"Fifty cents."

"And, uh, how much for a Mars?"

"Forty-five."

"What about a Snickers?"

"Christ, kid, the prices are listed. Pick one ya can afford and be done with it."

I glanced at Hawk. He was in the liquor section with his hip out, trying to pocket a jug of wine. I snickered into my palm. Larry smashed his fists down and shot up.

"What the hell do ya think yer doin', young man?" he yelled.

---

[10] Steal cigarettes. (See Hans Joseph Fellmann, *Chuck Life's a Trip*, Russian Hill Press, 2019.)

[11] Alcohol.

Hawk stood motionless. The jug bulged from his pant leg. He reached up and grabbed the first thing his fingers touched.

"Getting snacks," he said.

"Yeah? Well, I doubt those Tampons are gonna taste very good. Same goes for that two-dollar bottle'a rotgut in yer pocket. Now put 'em both back, and you kids get the hell outta here."

We knew Larry had a gun behind the counter. We did what he said. I smacked Hawk in the shoulder outside.

"Awesome plan."

We rode to his house. Hawk held a finger to his lips and opened the front door. He closed it quietly behind us. The doorknob clicked.

"Clarence, is that you?" his mother Sue shouted.

"Ugh, yes, bitch."

"Get in here and bring me my Valium!"

He marched into his mother's room. I heard the rattling of pills then a loud bang. A flurry of cusswords ensued. Hawk walked out and slammed the door.

"Now leave us alone," he yelled.

We made for the kitchen. A figure blocked our path. Its arms were folded, and its face was scarred. Its bullethead was freshly shaved.

"What's the problem, ladies?"

Hawk rolled his eyes.

"Fuck off, Duke."

Duke tackled his younger brother. Limbs flailed and popped. They rolled to a stop with Duke on top. He ripped off Hawk's shades.

"You wanna gimme a real answer?"

"We're pissed 'cuz Mom was bugging us," Hawk whined. "Plus, we tried to steal alcohol from Larry's but the fucker caught us. We wanted to get drunk tonight. What's it to you, anyways?"

Duke raised his eyebrows.

"I think it's time I show you faggots something."

He led us into the kitchen. He rounded the counter and stopped. He raised his hand at the back corner.

"And?" Hawk said.

Duke made a fist and jabbed it against the wood. A little door cracked open. He reached down and pulled it wide. Our eyes widened too. Bottles of every shape and color were stacked across neon blue shelves. It was a glowing treasure trove of booze. My wiener twitched. I reached for a bottle with both hands. Duke cuffed my wrists with two fingers.

"That's tequila. You start with this."

He picked up a bottle of raspberry wine. I crinkled my nose.

"In case you didn't know, I'm Mexican. I'll take the tequila."

He shrugged and let go of my wrists. I twisted off the cap and held the bottle to my lips. He looked at me and grunted.

"You ain't *that* Mexican with that fuckin' name of yours."

His words stung. I lifted the bottle and sucked. Tequila sloshed down my throat. My eyes welled with tears. I chugged and chugged. I kissed off and placed the bottle neatly on the counter.

"Howzat?"

"Beginner's luck."

I grabbed another bottle. This time it was Jägermeister.[12]

"You're fuckin' crazy, Felm,"[13] Hawk said.

I took down half the remaining Jäger. I did the same

---

[12] German alcoholic post-meal digestive aid or *degestif* made with 56 herbs and spices.

[13] Commonly used nickname for yours truly.

with the Mad Dog[14] and Goldschläger.[15] My stomach was hard with liquid. My smile was even harder. Duke grabbed a bottle and walked away.

"Whatever, ya dumb beaner."

Hawk and I shrugged off our encounter with Duke. We finished drinking and stumbled to the game room. Hawk stuck in *Street Fighter II*.[16] He fired it up and sat back. The characters twirled on the screen. I pointed my finger and laughed. My laughter turned into a burp. The burp provoked a loud rumble. My abdomen shook like a swimming pool in an earthquake. I rushed to the toilet and knelt. I opened my mouth and screamed. A shower of black chowder came out. Hawk ran into the bathroom. I was doubled over in my mess.

"Clarence," Sue yelled. "What's going on in there?"

"Nothing, bitch," he called back.

I heard plodding down the hall. Sue arrived at the threshold, panting. She was wearing a white kimono that could have doubled as a Jeep cover. Her bulbous face was bright red.

"You wouldn't have been lying if I'd asked you how much puke he'd made into the fucking toilet. Now, go in my room and get my big orange bottle."

Hawk scoffed and left. He returned and handed her the bottle. She removed the cap and took out a pill.

"Here," she said.

I reached up shakily and picked it from her fingers. It was long, white, and thick. I aimed it toward my mouth.

---

[14] American fortified wine whose alcohol content varies by flavor from 13% to 18%.

[15] Swiss cinnamon schnapps with thin but visible flakes of gold floating in it.

[16] Second installment in *Street Fighter*—a series of competitive fighting games developed by Capcom. *Street Fighter II* was released in North America for Super Nintendo in August 1992.

She grabbed my wrist.

"It doesn't go there."

"Huh?"

I dropped the pill in shock. Sue bent over hissing and picked it up. She yanked my pants down and spread my cheeks.

"Don't worry. I was a nurse."

She pressed the pill into my ass with her thumb. I gagged and puked again. The pill fired out and hit the wall. Sue cursed and grabbed it. This time she really drove it in. I craned my neck, saw stars, and blacked out.

I woke up fourteen hours later. My extremities were paralyzed. My stomach was a barrel of swamp water. My head was a throbbing nerve. My parents had to pick me up. Sue told them I'd eaten some funky pizza. They eyed her suspiciously and put me and my bike in the van. I groaned the whole way to my grandmother's.

The party was in full swing. I staggered inside and flopped on the couch. One of my uncles glanced at me. He cracked a beer and sat next to me.

"Little hair of the dog?"

I wasn't sure what he meant. I grabbed the bottle anyway. I looked right then left. I took a small sip. My headache started to split. My limbs felt light and fuzzy. I took another sip, then another, and another.

YARDWORK

e sat on a picnic bench scoping our next victim. Dozens of them littered the schoolyard of Sunshine Elementary like injured deer after a redneck shoot-off. We ran through our old targets: the tubby kid with the man tits and buck teeth, the skinny kid with the bowl cut and crooked feet, the stubby kid with no neck and thighs for hips, and the swishy kid with long eyelashes and dick-sucking lips. Tormenting them bored us. We needed fresh meat. We thought of a kid that had eluded us as of yet. His name was Finn Cecil, and he was a mark if he was a day old. He had the squint of a crying infant around clear blue eyes, blond curls like dried macaroni noodles, and skin the color of breast milk. He wore striped socks and Velcro sneakers. He walked buns out with his shoulders hunched and had scabs on his knees from playing t-ball. He was a member of every nerdy afterschool club in the book. He'd skipped a grade, meaning he was fourth-y posing as fifth. We wanted his ass so bad we could taste it. Alas, his mouth was fused to the booby of our resident yard duty, Ruth.

We spotted him on the basketball court hugging her bony legs and squealing. She looked at him over her bespectacled schnoz and chuckled. Some shit had gone down in the Timeout Zone; one kid left his red-painted square and punched another. The second kid punched back, and a fight ensued. Ruth stepped out of the loop of

Finn's arms and ran over there. We saw our chance. Norman jumped up and spun around.

"Y'all ready to get this little faggot?" he said.

The sweetness of evil seeped through my stomach. I looked at my compadres. Mason was stroking his incipient goatee and frowning villainously. Tim was cracking his big knuckles and twitching at the neck. Hawk was already bouncing on his heels. He shook his gorilla arms and ran his fingers through his bleached flattop.

"Chea, I'm ready," he grunted.

Norman smiled. His hair grew spikes and his freckles glinted. He zeroed in on me with his black eyes.

"What about you, Johann?"

I dipped my chin like, "What the fuck." He nodded and turned around. We followed him up the lot. Hawk marched out front and balled his fists. Finn saw us and his eyes widened. He covered his crotch and made an X with his legs. He looked over his shoulder at Ruth. She was chasing one kid while the other made fart noises and flicked his dick tip. Finn looked back at us and gulped. He uncrooked his legs and split. He ran past the jungle gym and into the tire park. He jumped in the mouth of the last tire and took refuge in its lip. We walked to the park's edge and stopped. We grabbed rocks and waited. A minute passed. Finn lifted his face above the rubber line. His eyes caught mine. He stuck out his tongue and sneered. Norman broke into laughter. It slashed at my skin like a steel whip. I cocked back my arm and let the rock fly. It zipped past Finn's curls and bounced away. I heard the rattling blow of Ruth's whistle. I rolled my eyes and huffed.

Me and my homies were suspended for a week. Finn stapled his gums to Ruth's asshole thereafter. We taunted him from the sidelines for the rest of the year. It wasn't enough to satisfy our urges. We graduated and parted ways; we went to one middle school and Finn went to another. We tabled revenge for a spell. We focused on other things like jacking hood ornaments and stealing booze, pilfing cigarettes and playing bloody knuckles[17] and getting high and drunk under creek bridges. We also developed a penchant for "TP-ing." To us, this meant more than dressing someone's front yard with toilet paper; we often combined it with car-keying, tire-slashing, lewd graffiti, and stink bombs. If we really wanted to get a motherfucker, we might finish by pounding on their front door at four in the morning, then hopping behind the bushes to watch their face when they saw our work.

On a Monday at the start of eighth grade, we were posted at the cafeteria. We were eating our cardboard hotdogs and plotting our next move. Outta nowhere, a ghost walked into the room. He was older and taller, but still a runt. His curls were longer and darker. His lactose face was covered in zits. He wore a Sharks[18] hoodie and skinny jeans. He was surrounded by the dorks from the Yearbook Club. I could hear him explaining how the Yearbook Club at his previous school was run. I realized this was the first time I'd heard Finn speak. His voice was high-pitched and warbly. He sounded like a mix of Mickey Mouse and Elmer Fudd. For every word he uttered, I wanted to smack a zit off his face. I turned to my homies to see what was good. Norman was tickling his fingertips together.

"Let's find out where he lives," he said.

Tim and I took care of the task. We waited for Finn after school on our bikes. He came out the multipurpose room a couple hours later. He said goodbye to his dork friends and grabbed his Huffy.[19] He pedaled down the

---

[17] A game in which two players take turns punching each other's knuckles with maximum force. Rotation continues until a player flinches, bleeds, or quits due to excessive pain.

[18] Professional ice hockey team from San Jose, California.

[19] Bicycle company founded by George P. Huffman in 1892, with headquarters in Dayton, Ohio. In the 90s, Huffy was considered by many kids to be one of the nerdiest brands of bikes.

road, whistling. We crept from behind the bushes and followed. He turned left at the stop sign and went down the Ave. He blew through the first light and went right at the second. I was surprised he didn't notice us. Tim was in his XXL Top Dawg[20] tee and baggy jeans, and I was in my blue Ben Davis[21] shirt and Dickies[22] with my belt hung low and my hair slicked back.

We tailed Finn to the outskirts of South Livermore. He cut right before the hills and into our hood. He rode down the street that led to mine. He went past parks we kicked it at and houses we'd hit and all sorts of familiar shit. A hundred feet before my turnoff, he stopped. He pedaled up the driveway of a big, red house with a three-car garage. He parked his bike on the porch and went inside. I shook my head and rubbed my eyes. He was under our noses the whole time. The only reasons we weren't privy were dumb luck, different tastes, and separate school routes. We took note of his cars, his neighbors, his yard. He had two tall trees and plenty of hedges. A sedan and a minivan were parked in his driveway. A fence ran along his property line, obstructing the view. It was too sweet to be true. We agreed to tell the others the next day.

Tim went one way, and I went the other. I pulled up at my house before dusk. I stuck my bike in the side yard and went inside. My mom sat at the kitchen table doing

---

[20] 90s clothing company that produced T-shirts embossed with cartoon caricatures of aggressive-looking dogs, and cheesy, sports-related quotes.

[21] American workwear brand, founded in 1935 and based in San Francisco, California. The clothing is popular among Chicano (i.e. Mexican-American) youth. Ben Davis shirts were shown in the music videos for the songs "Let Me Ride" (1992) by rapper Dr. Dre, and "Real Muthaphuckkin G's" (1993) by rapper Eazy-E.

[22] Subsidiary of Williamson-Dickie Mfg. Co., which is an apparel manufacturing company founded in Fort Worth, Texas, in 1922 by C. N. Williamson and E. E. "Colonel" Dickie, who began a denim bib overall company selling workwear to farm and ranch hands around the Southwest. Like Ben Davis, Dickies clothing is popular among Chicano youth.

the bills. She looked at me over the rim of her glasses.

"School ended hours ago. Where were you?"

I opened the fridge and pulled out a gallon of milk. I popped off the cap with my thumb and chugged.

"Ugh. Riding around," I gurgled.

I put back the milk and closed the fridge. My mother stared at me.

"Your father will be home soon. We'll see what you have to tell him."

A thread of fear ran up my heart. I shrugged it off and went to my room. I clicked on my CD player and slipped in *Black Sunday*.[23] The opening horns lulled me into a state. I faced my door mirror and lowered my chin. The bass dropped, and I raised my eyes. I put my shoulders on swing and twisted my fingers. B-Real[24] got on the mic and did the chorus. I sang, "I wanna get hiiiiiigh, soooo hiiiiiigh," along with him. We broke into spit at the same time. I heard my mother yell, "Turn that shit down." I ignored her and turned it up. I went deep, *deep* into the zone. I rapped through the first two tracks without missing a beat. I heard the front door squeak open, and my mother curse. I dipped my head and prepared for the next verse. It came through loud and crisp:

"Who you try'na get crazy wit, *ese*? Don'chu know I'm loco?"

The horns squealed and the bass dropped. I shook my head frenetically. I looked up to catch my reflection. I saw my giant, Germanic father standing in the doorway. His arms were folded, and his eyes narrowed. His mouth was

---

[23] Second studio album by American hip hop group Cypress Hill. It was released in 1993 and went triple platinum in the US with 3.4 million units sold.

[24] Louis Mario Freese (born June 2, 1970), aka "B-Real," is one of two lead rappers in Cypress Hill, along with "Sen Dog." He was born to a Mexican father and a Cuban mother. At 17, he was shot in the lung with a hollow-point .22 caliber bullet. He has been a longtime advocate of marijuana legalization and use.

an angry cut at the center of his beard. I froze in place and clenched my jaw. He stepped forward and pointed. His finger moved past me like a steel beam. It slammed against my CD player and shut off the song. He eyed me again and turned on his heel.

"Dinner's in ten minutes," he said.

I took a deep breath and steeled my nerves. I went to the bathroom and washed my face. I heard my sister's door open and her feet patter away. I toweled off and went into the kitchen. Everyone was at the table: my father at the head, my mother to his right, and my sister at the far end. My seat was to my father's left. I took it and looked at dinner. My mom had made *chilaquiles*[25] and whole beans—one of the few Mexican meals my father would eat. My mom said grace and we started. My father lifted a tortilla strip to his lips.

"Your mother tells me you came home late from school today. Mind tellin' me what that was about?"

He mouthed the strip and chewed. I shrugged.

"After-school stuff."

"Oh, extracurriculars?" he said, crunching. "Must mean your grades are gonna be stellar this year."

In seventh grade, I'd made five Cs and a D. My folks were none too pleased. I bunched my mouth and nodded.

"F'sheez."

He scowled and continued eating. I took a few bites and stood. He glared at me.

"A bee sting your ass?"

"No."

"Then what do you say?"

"Can I go now?"

"Come again?"

---

[25] Traditional Mexican dish of lightly fried tortilla strips often topped with a combination of refried beans, cheese, sour cream, sliced avocados, shredded chicken or beef, and green or red salsa. This dish is usually served at breakfast but can be eaten at any meal.

"May I be excused?"

"May I be excused?"

"May I be excused, please?"

"Yes. And you may also do the dishes. It's your turn."

I dropped my shoulders and hung my head. I gathered everyone's crap and dumped it in the sink. I washed and scrubbed and rinsed and stacked. My father poked his nose in every so often to make sure I was doing a proper job. I ignored him and finished. I went to my room, but not before being reminded that tomorrow was trash day, and the following was lawn day. I gave it a "Yeah, yeah," and closed my door. I clicked on my music and tried to reenter the zone. I heard three quick knocks. I paused "Insane in the Brain" and barked, "What?" My father opened the door slowly.

"Can I come in?" he asked.

"I guess."

He entered my space like a diffuse nebula: big, boundless, and full of gas, but benevolent just the same. He glanced at the new posters on my wall. They were of grimacing rap stars with gold chains, fancy cars with foreign names, and pretty ladies with boobs for brains and long tan legs. He gave each one an appropriate nod and sat on my bed. It squeaked miserably and sagged under his weight. I pulled out my desk chair and sat across from him. He rested his elbows on his knees and looked at me.

"How's it goin?" he asked.

"Good."

"You likin' eighth grade?"

"Sure."

"Make any new friends?"

"Not really."

"That's too bad 'cuz some of those yahoos you hang out with are nothing but—"

"Dad."

"Sorry. Anyways, you know I was on business in Osaka."[26]

"Yeah."

"Well, I brought you these."

He reached in his shirt pocket and pulled out a few postcards. He handed them to me with a little smile. I took them and looked them over. They were covered with golden pagodas and snowcapped mountains and samurai castles. Something stirred in my marrow. It was strange, but it felt good. I thanked my father. He nodded and stood.

"No problem."

He walked out and closed my door. I put the postcards on my desk and turned on the song. It didn't hit the same way. I rapped through it, watched TV, and fell asleep. I woke up the next morning and cut to school. I snored until lunchtime. I went to the cafeteria and copped a turd sandwich. I took it to the big bench my homies were at. Tim and I gave the scoop on Finn's crib. We got to the part about the big front yard and Norman grinned.

"Baumish.[27] Let's hit him up this weekend."

We agreed. We drafted the ultimate TP job to be carried out that Saturday at 3:00 a.m. We avoided Finn the rest of the week so as not to alert him. We gathered toilet paper, shaving cream, pocketknives, and other goodies, and stashed 'em in secret spots. Hawk crashed at Norman's as he lived up the way. Mason and Tim crashed at mine that Friday. We watched movies till our folks and siblings were catching Z's. We grabbed our supply sacks and crept out wearing beanies and black hoodies. We met in the cul-de-sac behind my house. We took inventory one last time, then hit the night.

It was cool and still and dark. The streets were long

---

[26] Japanese city of 2.7 million people in the Kansai region of Honshu. It is the country's third-largest city, and a major center of culture, food, and finance.

[27] Great; awesome; excellent; delicious (when referring to food).

graves, the trees were silent goons, and the sky was a giant gangster mouth flecked with diamonds. We shuffled up the block and around the corner. We posted at the edge of Finn's yard and scoped the scene. Everything was peaceful and serene: the trees, the lawn, the hedges, the fence, the cars, the steps, and the house were covered in a sheen of blue moondust. We rubbed our mitts together and wiggled our fingers. We reached into our bags and pulled out two rolls each. We split 'em at the seams and got to hockin'. They flew up—way up—in the branches and came down in beautiful white daddy-longlegs. We threw ten, twenty, a hundred times. We wrapped the trunks like mummies and the hedges like Christmas presents. We tossed the rollers every which way. We went back to our bags and grabbed the shaving cream. Tim, Norman, and I scrawled the garage. Hawk tagged the porch, and Mason did the fence. We wrote things like, "Fuck you, Finn" and "Eat a dick." I'm pretty sure Hawk drove it home by drawing a big veiny boner with a jizzing tip. We chuckled and brought out the dog shit. We sprinkled it over the steps and down the walkway. We stuck a load under the doormat. We stomped it into the concrete and pissed on it for good measure. We reached in our pockets and pulled out our blades. We stabbed the tires on each car and knifed the doors. We found Finn's bike and twisted it into a pretzel. We dumped the garbage cans on the driveway and over the grass. We stood back and admired our work. It looked like Pollock[28]

---

[28] American painter (January 28, 1912 – August 11, 1956). Lead figure in the abstract expressionist movement. He was most famous for his "drip technique" during which he poured or splashed liquid paint onto a horizontal surface, thus enabling him to view and paint his canvases from all angles. Although he was most recognized for his paintings, Jackson Pollock's first love was sculpting. He took classes in clay modeling and stone carving in his late teens and early twenties in Greenwich Village. In a letter to his father, he wrote, "Cutting in stone holds my interest deeply. I like it better than painting."

had sculpted *Guernica*[29] with the rubble of exploded bathrooms. We fixed our beanies and grinned. Somewhere under our shoes, the Devil clapped.

We woke up at noon the next day. My mom made scrambled eggs and tortillas, my pops flipped through the paper, and Mason, Tim, and I pretended like everything was A-okay. We wolfed down our food with Sunny Delight[30] and whole milk. We piled into the family room and played *Mortal Kombat II*[31] and argued over which fatality was the best. My folks took my sister to a friend's house and ran errands; they said they'd be back around six. Me and my homies ripped each other's heads off for a few hours. We never really talked about the job. It was almost as if we hadn't done it—like demons had borrowed our skinsuits and done it for us.

Mason and Tim split at five. I went to my bedroom to unwind. I slipped on my headphones and lay in my soft coffin. I closed my eyes and let Dre[32] and Snoop[33] speak

---

[29] Large oil-on-canvas painting by Spanish artist Pablo Picasso. It exhibits the suffering, violence, and chaos brought about by the 1937 bombing of the Spanish-Basque town of Guernica by Nazi-Germany and Fascist Italy at the behest of Spanish Nationalists. Many consider it to be one of the most powerful antiwar paintings in history.

[30] Tangy, orange-flavored drink developed by Doric Foods. It contains less than 2% fruit juice and is now known as SunnyD.

[31] Second installment in the ultraviolent *Mortal Kombat* videogame series. MKII featured improved gameplay, an expanded mythos, more gruesome fatalities, and new characters such as Kitana, Mileena, Kung Lao, Noob Saibot, and the series' recurring villain, Shao Kahn.

[32] Andre Romelle Young (born February 18, 1965), known professionally as Dr. Dre, is an American rapper, beat-maker, record producer, and business mogul. He is the CEO and founder of Aftermath Entertainment and Beats Electronics, and previously co-founded, co-owned, and was the president of Death Row Records. Dre's solo debut studio album, *The Chronic* (1992), released under Death Row Records, made him one of the best-selling American music artists of 1993.

[33] Calvin Cordozar Broadus Jr. (born October 20, 1971), known professionally as Snoop Dogg, is an American rapper, songwriter, media personality, actor, and businessman. He was featured heavily on Dr. Dre's debut solo album, *The Chronic*. His own debut solo album,

the truth. I heard three knocks. I lifted my lids and yelled, "What?" My father pushed open the door. He wore an expression like cancer had visited.

"Would you come to the kitchen, please."

I blew through my teeth and removed my headphones. I stood and walked out. He and my mother sat at the table. They both had the same sorry face. I worried our dog Tommy had been hit by a car. I sat and asked what the problem was. My mother looked at my father with long eyes. He cleared his throat.

"We drove past the Cecils' house on our way home from the Tennis Club. It looked like a bomb hit the place."

My cheeks went numb.

"What's that hafta do with me?"

"Johann, please," my mother said. "We know you and your friends pick on Finn. His mother, Bonnie, and I have attended plenty of PTO[34] meetings together. She's told me a lot."

"That doesn't mean we did shit last night."

"Who said anything about last night?" my father asked.

"Or today, or whenever."

"Cut the crap. Your mother just got off the phone with Tim's mother. Apparently, he'd told her you guys were gonna go TP-ing and she bought him the damn toilet paper."

I felt the walls closing in. My face reddened like a baby in a gas chamber. I grabbed a napkin and wiped the sweat from my brow. I steadied my expression and looked at my pops.

Doggystyle, produced by Dr. Dre, was released by Death Row Records in November 1993, and went quadruple platinum. Its hit singles "What's My Name?" and "Gin & Juice" are hip hop classics.

[34] Parent Teacher Organization (PTO) is a formal organization comprised of parents, teachers, and school staff. Its general goals include volunteerism of parents, encouragement of teachers and students, community involvement, and the welfare of students and families.

"Am I in trouble?"

"In a way," he said, smirking.

"Whaddaya mean?"

"I'll let you think on it. Tell me what you come up with tomorrow."

I went to my room and thought on it. I did this by way of watching Nick at Nite[35] until my folks told me to turn it off. I got in my PJs and hit the light. I lay in bed and stared at the ceiling and let the glowing green star-stickers carry me off. I thought about the job and how it made me feel, about Finn and his family and the whole shebang. I decided I didn't give a shit. TP-ing wasn't murder—it was fun, and if I hadn't gotten caught, I'da done it again. I knew I couldn't tell this to my pops. I had to come up with an appropriate punishment that would make him feel like he'd laid down the law but would afford me the opportunity to sneak off and smoke cigarettes with my buds. I came up with the perfect thing. I told him over pancakes and bacon the next morning.

"You can ground me for two weeks and give me extra yardwork. I'll even rake the leaves and prune the bushes."

He smiled delicately.

"I see you've thought really hard about this."

"I have. Anyways, I thought you wanted me to come up with a punishment for myself."

"Son, I can ground you for two years and make you do yardwork till your hands fall off. But that won't make you get the point."

"Okay, what's the point?"

"You'll find out tonight."

I rolled my eyes and finished breakfast. I went to my

---

[35] American nighttime programming block that broadcasts on the Nickelodeon channel. It primarily appeals to adult and older youth audiences, though it is not as risqué or violent as other services targeting a similar audience. Back in the mid-90s, its popular shows included *Taxi*, *Bewitched*, *I Love Lucy*, and *The Bob Newhart Show*.

room and plopped on my bed. I didn't know what the old man was babbling about. I didn't care either. I passed the day thumbing through my stash of dirty magazines. I heard those three miserable knocks at eight. I stood and opened the door. My father was in his blue jeans and windbreaker.

"Let's go," he said.

I huffed and grabbed my hoodie. I slipped it on and followed him outside. We got in the Aerostar[36] and pulled outta the driveway. We turned right and went up the block. I thought we might be going to Tim's house. My pops passed the turnoff. I asked him where we were headed. He didn't respond. We came to the stop sign and turned left. We parked halfway up the hill. Finn's house was across the street. The yard was cleaned, and the fence and windows were washed. The tires on the cars were still flat. A few tendrils of toilet paper blew from the trees. I looked at my pops and shrugged. He turned off the engine and waited. A minute later, a station wagon arrived. Tim got out and stood on the sidewalk. I asked my dad what the hell was going on. He pointed to Finn's front door.

"You're gonna go up there and apologize to that poor kid and his family. Then you're gonna ask them if there's anything you can do to make up for the shit you pulled."

I could see in his eyes that he meant it—that if I curled one lip or rolled one eyeball, he'd march me up there by the nape of my neck and ring the doorbell himself. I took a deep breath and got out of the car. I walked across the street to Tim. He was in a similar state; I could tell this wasn't his idea either. We turned and faced the walkway. What had once seemed like a slice of *Candyland*[37] was now

---

36 Minivan manufactured by Ford from 1986 to 1997. It was the first minivan produced by Ford and it derived its name from its slope-nosed "one-box" exterior.

37 Children's board game published by Hasbro. The game requires no reading, strategy, or decision-making, and only minimal counting skills. The race is woven around a storyline about finding King Kandy,

a path to the guillotine. We stepped up it with lead in our guts. The trees and bushes and cars faded. The house got bigger and redder and scarier. I reminded myself that Finn lived there, and not *It*.[38]

We arrived at the front door. A light clicked on and showered us with dusty rays. We stood in place like two crooks in a lineup. I reached out and rang the bell. It clanged and warbled. I heard the sound of footsteps. I tried to look emotionless. A man opened the door. He was shorter than my father but taller than me. He had hay-colored hair and a thick brown mustache. He wore glasses, shorts, and a T-shirt. I noticed a tattoo of a shamrock on his forearm. A woman stood behind him. She had gray curls and a double chin. Her face was scarlet from crying. It was hard to look at. The man asked us who we were. The woman twisted her mouth and pointed over his shoulder.

"That's Maria's son, Johann," she screamed. "He and his gang are the ones who bully Finn and destroyed our property."

The man steadied himself. He looked at me, then at Tim, then back at me.

"This true?" he asked.

"Yeah," I said.

"Okay. What are you here for?"

I opened my mouth to answer. The woman got in my face.

"He's here to say he's sorry for the mess he's caused," she yelled. "Isn't that right, Johann?"

---

the lost king of Candyland, through locations such as Candy Cane Forest and Gumdrop Mountain.

[38] Horror novel written in 1986 by American author Stephen King. The story follows the experiences of seven children as they are terrorized by an evil entity that disguises itself as their greatest fears in order to hunt them. "It" primarily appears in the form of Pennywise the Dancing Clown, who wears a frilled outfit and has red hair, a red nose, orange eyes, and razor-sharp fangs.

The man patted the air.

"Bonnie, please," he said.

"Don't 'please' me, Frank," she spat. "Those boys are lucky we haven't called the police."

She turned and stomped away. I heard her sobbing. I wondered where Finn was. Frank raised his eyebrows.

"Where's the rest of your crew?" he asked.

"Prolly at home," Tim said.

"You boys come here of your own mind or did your folks make you?"

"Our folks made us," I said.

"Well, it was still big of you."

"Thanks. And we're sorry for what we did."

"Yeah," Tim seconded. "We're really sorry."

Frank looked us both in the eyes. We resisted the urge to flinch. He held our gaze for a small eternity. Then he bent his lip.

"Did you hafta put dog shit under my doormat?"

We didn't know whether to laugh or run. We stood dumbfounded. He thinned his eyes.

"Anyways, it's fine. Apology accepted. Have a good night."

He closed the door and clicked off the light. Tim and I blinked in the dark. We walked down to the curb and said late. Tim got in the station wagon with his folks and bounced. I crossed the street and got in the Aerostar. My father looked at me.

"How'd it go?"

"Fine."

"They accept your apology?"

"More or less."

"How 'bout making up for what you did? They come up with something?"

"Nope."

"That's alright. I can think of plenty."

TURBO SAL

Sal pulled up to my house in his new car. It was a Ford Probe GT Turbo,[39] grey with chrome rims. He clicked off the engine and stepped out. A cigarette dangled from his lips.

"What'cha think?" he said.

"It's baumish. When'd you get it?"

"Today. Wanna go for a cruise?"

"Chea hea."[40]

I told my folks I'd be back in a few. I slid into the car and shut the door. The interior was velvety red. It reeked of cigarettes and pine. Sal climbed in and started the engine. A swarm of mechanical hornets exploded from the hood. He slammed his door and grinned.

"You ready to fuckin' get it?"[41] he said.

He shifted into first and released the clutch. The wheels squealed and the car jerked. We shot down the street. Trees streaked by my window like green rain. We whipped around the corner and onto the open road. Sal shifted from first to second to third. Phone poles bent around us. Stop signs melted and streetlights cracked. Passersby dropped their jaws. We were the fastest damn thang Livermore ever saw.

---

[39] Liftback coupé produced by Ford from 1988 until 1997. It had a turbocharged, intercooled V6 engine with 145 hp and 190 lb-ft of torque.

[40] Yes; Absolutely.

[41] Get a cock in your ass; Get fucked.

We blazed around for an hour then stopped at Sal's. His twin brother Jessup was smoking on the porch. He got up and checked the ride.

"Where'd ya find this piece'a shit?"

Sal ripped the cigarette from his lips.

"It's better'n yer fuckin' Jetta."[42]

"No way man, the Jetta's got style. This thing's barely got paint."

"It's supposed to be grey, fool."

"Whatever."

We went inside and hit the game room. We popped in *Top Gear Rally*.[43] The selection screen appeared.

"I'm not seein' the Turbo," Jessup said.

Sal grunted. "It's right next to the Jetta. Oh shit, never mind. That's a booger on the screen."

"My ass, faggot."

The twins went back and forth. Sal threw down his controller and left. I followed him. We went to his car. Jessup came out.

"You should cruise to the Blue Moon Saloon and pick up some bitches," he yelled.

"Fuck off," Sal yelled back. "The Turbo may have some wear and tear but at least it has balls. Your pussy-ass car prolly came with a dress."

Jessup's face turned strawberry red. He shouted an insult at the top of his lungs. Sal clipped it in half with his door. He twisted the key and sparked the engine.

"Let's get the fuck outta here."

---

[42] Compact car manufactured by Volkswagen since 1979. The sedan came with two or four doors and seated four or five. Because it could be used as a small family car and was frequently driven by women, it was often referred to as a "bitch car" by boys in Livermore.

[43] Racing video game developed in 1997 by Boss Game Studios for Nintendo 64. It features a championship mode where a single player must complete various races, and a multiplayer mode where two players may compete against each other via a split-screen display.

We cut back into town. The sun dropped behind the hills and scared up the night. It hung in the sky like a tarantula on a string. Its millions of blinking eyes stared down at us. Sal drove and puffed his cigarette. The smoke curled around his wrist and threaded out the window. The streets were empty. We sped with impunity. At the end of town, we hit a red light. We pulled up to the crosswalk and stopped. A noise caught our ears. We looked right and saw a car. It was a janky blue Supra[44] with black trim. Its driver was hanging out the window. He had a backward hat and big biceps. He slapped his door and bounced his eyebrows.

"This fucker wants to go," Sal said.

Biceps flicked his tongue and revved his engine. Sal blew smoke at him and revved back. I tightened my belt and gritted my teeth. The light clicked green, and we shot forward. Everything stretched and blurred. Sal got a nose on the guy and kept it through the intersection and down the hill. We rounded the first corner. I looked over at Biceps. He was laughing wildly and flashing the devil horns. Our lanes began to merge. We rounded the second corner and saw an oncoming car. Sal couldn't get over. I screamed at him to let Biceps pass.

"Fuck that asshole," he said.

Sal gunned it. Biceps gunned it too; he tried to squeak ahead of us before the gap closed. His front wheel twisted inwards, and he zipped away. A turnoff was ahead of him. He missed it and hit a brick wall. I watched his head bang against the steering wheel. It exploded like a hot watermelon. His car scrunched together and dropped. I turned to Sal.

"That guy fucking gottem,"[45] I screamed.

---

[44] Three-door liftback sports car manufactured by Toyota from 1978 to 1986, then again from 2019 to present (2021). The 1986 model had a 6-cylinder engine with 161 hp and 169 lb-ft of torque.

[45] To get them (multiple cocks) in the ass; to get butt-fucked by

Sal looked over his shoulder then back at the road. His eyes were solid glass.

We pulled up at my house. I ran inside and to my parents' room. I pushed open the door. My parents were in bed asleep.

"You guys," I yelled. "Sal and I just saw a horrible accident."

My Dad snorted himself awake. He was naked except for his underwear. He rubbed his eyes.

"What exactly happened?"

"We were kinda racing. And the other guy slammed into a brick wall."

"You were *kind of* racing. Did you call the cops?"

"No."

"Did you go back and help?"

"No."

"What *did* you do?"

"Came here and told you. I think he's dead, Dad."

"Jesus Christ."

He put on his bathrobe, and we got in the Aerostar. We drove to the street where the accident had happened. Red lights were blinking in the distance. We pulled up to them slowly. A fire truck and an ambulance were on the curb. A cop car was off to one side. The Supra was scrunched in the middle. Biceps was nowhere in sight.

"Maybe he made it," I said.

"It's possible," my dad said.

We turned around and drove home. The next day we checked the papers. We saw no mention of any auto-related fatalities. I felt a little better.

A few months passed. Sal and I never spoke of the

---

many dicks; to make a really big mistake; to be doing something really poorly; to be in a really poor state; to have something really bad happen to you; to die. Often abbreviated to "gettem" in the present and "gottem" in the past.

incident. It was almost as if we'd imagined it. Life returned to normal. One weekend, we went to a house party. Everyone was in the living room, drinking. Sal wandered off with some chick. I grabbed a beer and chatted. I heard someone yell. He was a guy I knew called T-Boss. He sounded like a greasy trumpet. He blew and blew. I tried to ignore him. Something caught me.

"Yeah, it happened like three months ago," he said to his buddy.

I turned and faced him.

"What did?" I asked.

"This accident I saw."

"Go on."

"Well, I was cruisin' along one night and I spotted an ambulance, so I pulled up and saw these paramedics standing in front of a totaled sports car, and there was this dude lying on the ground, and *man* this fucker was hit *bad*. His whole head was busted into pieces—straight bled through the sheet the second they put it over him."

My stomach juices curdled.

"Where was this?" I asked.

"Over near First Street."

"Was the car a blue Supra?"

"Yeah, how the fuck did you know?"

I pinched the bridge of my nose.

"'Cuz I was riding shotgun in the car it was racing."

"Dude, tell me what happened."

I told him the story. By the end, I was ready to puke. T-Boss slapped my thigh.

"You fuckin' rock," he said.

I nodded and walked off. I found Sal in the hallway. I told him I was out.

"Need a ride?" he asked.

"Nah man, I'm gonna call my pops."

Sal bore his grey teeth.

"Pussy."

LECTURES

I left my JC[46] and drove to my grandparents' rickety house at break. It was eighty degrees, and I was exhausted from having sat through lectures all morning. I schlepped up the steps and pushed open the door. My grandparents sat at the kitchen table, reading the newspaper and sipping coffee. I greeted them in Spanish. My grandpa folded down the corner of his paper and looked at me with one eye.

"The elections are tomorrow," he said.

I dropped my backpack and grabbed the chair farthest from him. I sat and rubbed the back of my neck.

"*¿Me oíste?*" he said. Did you hear me?

I asked my granny if we had any food. She nodded and said she'd make me an omelet.

"Who you gonna vote for?" my grandpa continued.

"I don't know."

"There's no question. You vote for Bush."[47]

I tightened my shoulders. Sweat beaded on my forehead.

"*Dime lo que estás pensando,*" he barked. Tell me what you're thinking.

---

[46] Abbreviation for Junior College.

[47] George Walker Bush (born July 6, 1946), also referred to as "George W" or simply "Bush," is an American politician, member of the Republican Party, and businessman who served as the 43rd president of the United States from 2001 to 2009. In the 2000 US elections, he ran against democrat Al Gore and won the electoral vote but not the popular vote, becoming the fourth person in history to be elected president in this manner.

"I am not voting for Bush," I said through clenched teeth.

He glared at me murderously.

"You mean to tell me you gonna vote for that *mayate*[48]-lovin' liberal?"

A spring blew. Years of repressed anger surged out of me like sour piss after a night of whiskey drinking.

"Fuck Gore,[49] too," I shouted. "I don't care if the son-of-bitch wins or not. But I'm not gonna sit here and let you fill my head with your bullshit anymore. I don't think like you. I never have and I never will."

I caught my breath and looked at him. His tongue had shriveled and his eyes had frozen. His pointed finger crumbled to ash. I brushed it from my shoes and left. The weather outside was cooler. The sun was prettier, and the air was fresh. Class was in twenty minutes. I got in my car and drove to the beach.

---

[48] Ethnic slur in Chicano slang which means "black person" or "nigger." The term comes from the Classical Nahuatl or "Aztec" word *mayātl*, which means "rhinoceros beetle." The rhinoceros beetle has a black exterior and is an invasive species to Mexico. The fact that Blacks and Chicanos often lived in adjacent neighborhoods and engaged in gang-related warfare, may account for the term's origin, meaning, and proliferation among Chicanos.

[49] Albert Arnold Gore Jr. (born March 31, 1948) is an American politician and environmentalist who served as the 45th US vice president from 1993 to 2001 under President Bill Clinton. Gore was the Democratic nominee for the 2000 presidential election. He won the popular vote by 547,398 votes, but lost the electoral vote 266 to 271, in favor of George W. Bush – the Republican nominee.

LAZY BOY

He throws back the door to his trailer and lumbers in. The smell of cigarettes and mildew fill his nostrils. He snorts it into his brainpan and cracks his neck. His nerves are especially shot today because he saw someone at the grocery store he works at, someone he knows from long ago. She was his old housekeeper in his old house—the one where the horror show that was his childhood unfolded.

He needs a hit bad. He dumps his keys on the dresser, peels off his sweaty work shirt, and tosses it on a pile of laundry. He kicks his massive frame around and plops in his La-Z-Boy.[50] He sits still for a second, gripping the arms of his seat. The moonlight comes through his blinds and covers his skin. The fruit juice stains on his forearms turn black. He looks down at himself. What was once a powerful body, sculpted by years of athletics, has fallen into disrepair. His pecs and biceps sag. His gut is distended and misshapen like a beat-up medicine ball. His only recognizable features from when he was the hero of our neighborhood are his blue eyes. But even their clarity has splintered and fogged.

He fishes around in the desk drawer and pulls out a

---

[50] American furniture manufacturer based in Monroe, Michigan. It makes upholstered recliners, sofas, stationary chairs, lift chairs, and sleeper sofas. Its recliners are considered by many to be the standard; so much so that the term "lazy boy" is often used to refer to any and all recliners.

pipe and lighter. He lifts the pipe to his flakey lips and sparks it. He sucks hard and the flame bends cartoonlike into the bowl. It bathes the crystals in fire and they singe and pop. The smoke collects in the bowl and curls up the stem. He inhales and releases the carb. The images torturing his mind blur. He no longer recognizes the large, matronly woman bleeding from the head at the end of his stairwell, nor the scar-faced bully with a pit bull's physique, screaming the name "Clarence" in an upturned, flaming Jeep. Hawk leans back on the bare springs of his recliner and grins. Soon the nightmares will all be a dream.

THE MOST BEAUTIFUL HAIR IN LIVERMORE

As a teen, I had the prettiest hair. It was long, black, and shiny. It belonged on a Vietnamese whore. I combed it in front of the mirror at night. It was shaved around the sides. I slicked it back and braided it down my shoulder. The kids at school called me Tecumseh.[51] The name stung, but I wore it with pride. In my senior year, I was voted best hair. I beat out all the Cholas[52] who groomed their manes for a living. I

---

[51] Shawnee chief and warrior (c. 1768 – October 5, 1813) who promoted inter-tribal unity and formed a Native American confederacy against the expansion of the United States. Although his efforts ended with his death in the War of 1812, he became an iconic folk hero in American, Indigenous, and Canadian popular history. Transliterations of his name from the Shawnee language include "I Cross the Way," and "Shooting Star." Like many Shawnee warriors, he wore his hair long on the top and shaved around the sides. In Germany, Tecumseh has long been admired. This is due in large part to popular novels by author Fritz Steuben, beginning with *The Flying Arrow* (1930). Steuben used Tecumseh to promote Nazi ideology. However, later editions of his novels removed the Nazi elements.

[52] Member of the Chicano subculture often associated with criminality, anti-social behavior, and gang activity. Cholo (male) style often includes a combination of the following: a flannel buttoned at the top over a white t-shirt, a hair net over slicked-back hair, a shaved head, a beanie or tied bandana pulled down just above the eyes, a reverse baseball cap, dark sunglasses, baggy khaki pants or shorts, gold chains, long socks pulled up to the knees, white sneakers, and religious tattoos. Chola (female) style often includes long white T-shirts, plaid shirts, baggy jeans, flat black shoes, long hair, spiked bangs, and dark eyeliner, lip liner, and lipstick. The term "Cholo" emerged in the early 17th century as a way for Spanish colonizers to denote a child with one mestizo parent and one Amerindian parent. It is a Windward

told my father and he laughed. I looked at his naked scalp and laughed back.

"At least I *have* hair," I said. "You're bald as a doorknob."

"Well, the apple doesn't fall far."

"Nuh-uh, I was reading that baldness is from the mother's side. And grandpa Papito has tons of hair."

He shrugged and walked left. I smirked and walked right. I went to the bathroom and took a shower. I noticed I had a few split ends. A little conditioner took care of it. I was a gorgeous Indian boy again.

A year and a bit passed. My split ends ate their way to my roots. My hair got rattier and rattier. It lost its deep black shine. I used a pricier conditioner to combat this. It worked for a time. One day, my locks were so tangled I could barely get a brush through them. I went to my mother and whined.

"Mom, my hair is fucked up."

She was reading *Chicken Soup for the Histrionic Boy's Soul.*[53] She looked at me over the rims of her glasses.

"What's the problem with it?"

"I don't know. It just looks shitty. And these split ends won't go away."

She put down her book and grabbed a lock of my hair. It crunched like a paper bag. She released it and grabbed her purse.

Islands Taino word, which means "dog of disreputable origin" or "mutt."

[53] American self-help book series published by motivational speakers Jack Canfield and Mark Victor Hansen in 1993. The *Chicken Soup for the Soul* book series consists of inspirational true stories about ordinary people's lives. The first book became a major best-seller because of its ability to change others' perspective on certain social topics. The books are widely varied, each with a different theme, such as kids, teens, angels, and miracles. There are no actual books in the series dedicated to young boys with Histrionic Personality Disorder (HPD), but there should be.

"I'm taking you to Shokoufeh."

"Who?"

We got in the car and drove downtown. We parked in front of the Livermore Post Office. A small, white building was across the street. The letters on the window read "Shokoufeh's Magical Fingers." I shook my head.

"I really hope this is a hair salon, Mom."

She laughed and waved me on. I followed her through the door. A tiny bell chimed.

"Vaan minoot," a woman in back yelled.

I thinned my eyes and looked around. I saw shelves and shelves of crystals. A few chairs with headrests were off to the side. They looked like they were from the nuthouse.

"Maw-ree-aw," the woman cried.

She parted a curtain of beads with her bony fingers. She floated through it and up to my mother. She wore a flowery kimono that drew out behind her. Her 'do was a nest of glistening curls. She kissed my mother on both cheeks. Her lipstick left the kisses in place. She walked to me and extended a hand covered in turquoise jewelry.

"And who is dis byootiful young boy?"

"This is my son, Johann," my mother said.

"Vell khelloooo, Jokhaan. Vat kan I do for you?"

"It's these split ends. They're ruining my hair."

"Oh?"

She ran her hands over my scalp. Her fingers were like spider legs. She fanned them to detangle my hair. I screamed in pain.

"Okay, dis is problem," she said. "But no verry, Shokoufeh vill cat hair and everything vill be perfect again."

"Cut my hair?"

She sat me down and put her fingers to work. She cleaned, combed, sliced, and styled while I watched my hair float to the ground. She finished, and I hardly recognized myself. I looked more like Phoebe Cates[54] than Tecumseh.

"You like?" she asked.

"Let's go with tolerate."

My mother chuckled and paid the bill. It was seventy dollars, plus tip. We thanked Shokoufeh and made for the door. She stopped us and handed me a little bottle.

"You vill also need my magical shampoo."

"For split ends?"

"Nooo, thinning hair."

"What?"

We drove home. I checked my head with a magnifying mirror. My hair was its normal thickness in the dark. I clicked on the light and half of it vanished.

"Holy shit," I cried.

I stripped off my clothes and jumped in the shower. I grabbed the magical shampoo and squirted it all over my head. It tingled at first. Then it burned. I cranked up the water. It washed away the suds. They ran down my legs and around my feet. I noticed something black near my toes. I reached down and fished it up. It was a cluster of my hair. I looked around the shower. It was littered with black strands. My heart sank and my knees buckled. I collapsed with a thud.

The weeks passed. My hair got thinner and thinner. I blew through my bottle of magical shampoo. It did nothing to slow the loss. I went out and bought thickening gels. I used them by the handful to style my hair. I toyed with a few different 'dos. I liked The Wave best. To make it, I brushed my hair toward the front. I combed it out and curled it around. If I did it just right, I could hide my huge

---

[54] American actress known for her roles in films such as *Fast Times at Ridgemont High*, *Gremlins*, and *Drop Dead Fred*. In the early 90s, she sported jaw-length, jet black hair.

forehead. This worked for a time. One evening, I sat down for dinner. My father looked at me and snorted.

"Gettin' a little thin up there," he said.

I flicked a pea at him. He blocked it with his hand and laughed. I threw down my cutlery and stormed off. I went to the bathroom and looked in the mirror. My wave was a wispy curl. I hung my head and sulked.

Knock. Knock. Knock.

"You okay in there?" my father asked.

"Yeah."

"Alright. When you finish, could you please see me in my bedroom?"

"Whatever."

I washed my face and went in there. He was sitting on the bed. A chair was facing him. I sat in it and folded my arms.

"I know what you're going through," he said.

"Bullshit," I spat. "You may notta had the nicest hair but at least you had it through your thirties. I'm barely in my twenties and look at me."

"I understand. But you can't let this beat you. I'm gonna do what I can to help."

"Right."

That weekend, he took me to a hair specialist; he was a sun-dried coot with a mess of hair plugs. He invited us into his office. Smiling blow-ups of his clientele were on the walls. He leaned back in his seat and formed a steeple with his fingers.

"So, what can I do you for?"

"My hair is thinning," I said. "I'm thinking of a transplant."

"Good man, let's have a look at your pattern."

He ran me through a series of tests. They involved little gadgets with big flashes. He reviewed the data.

"You're a type Six-A."

"What the hell does that mean?"

"It means if you don't have a transplant now and pair it with hair loss meds, you'll be bald by twenty-five."

"Oh my God. What's that gonna cost?"

"The meds are about a hundred bucks a month. And the procedure is about five grand."

"That's obscene."

"You wanna look good for the ladies, don't you?"

"I guess."

That night we had a family meeting. My father offered to spot me the cash if I paid him back in installments. I told him that would take me a lifetime delivering pizza. My mother raised her eyebrows.

"Why don't you shave your head?"

"Now there's a fuckin' plan."

"I'm serious, sweetie. It would look good. You were a cesarean baby. Your head is nice and round."

"Doesn't matter. I'll still look like a fuckin' lightbulb. There's no solution. I'm just gonna shoot myself."

I left the table and grabbed the phone. I went to my room and locked the door. I dialed my buddy, Kip. I told him the news and he laughed.

"Quit being a pussy and shave it. I've had mine shaved for years and I love it."

"You love it?"

"Absolutely. It's easier to manage and much cheaper. Furthermore, chicks go for guys with bald heads."

"Horseshit."

"Look at Vin Diesel and Jason Statham. They're bald and they get tons of girls."

"They're movie stars, genius."

"Oh *baaad*.[55] Come over tomorrow and I'll shave it."

---

[55] Fuck that; Fuck off; What-fuckin-ever; That's bullshit.

I barely slept. I woke up with a headache. I went to the bathroom and looked in the mirror. For a second, I saw my old hair. It was streaming over my shoulders like black milk. I smiled whimsically and ran my hands through it. It dissolved between my fingers. I was left staring at a sad, balding man. I turned and walked out. I got in my car and drove to Kip's. The music glugged from my speakers. The frown on my face bent deeper. I sank into the fabric of my seat. A loud bang snapped me up. I looked out and saw chaos.

"What the fuck?"

As I inched toward the intersection, I saw two cars. One had a smashed-in nose and the other a smashed-in side. Bystanders swarmed the wreckage. Some pulled the injured from their windows, and others called the police. A single man stood out. He was tall and tan with frizzy hair. He walked around in a daze. He saw something on the ground and his face shattered.

"My baby," he screamed.

He reached down and lifted the mangled infant. Its arm dangled from the cradle of his hands. I burst into tears. I parked around the corner so as not to crash. I took a minute to compose myself. I got out to see if I could help. An ambulance had arrived. A guy walking away from the scene approached me.

"I wouldn't go up there," he said.

"Why?"

"It's total carnage, man. Let the medics take care of it."

I turned and got in my car. I said a silent prayer. The streets were cold and empty. I forgot about my hair.

ONE-EIGHTY

finished my cheese pizza and hopped on the train. I picked a seat in back and glanced out the window. The mountains of Norway all looked the same. Sure, they were gorgeous with their green shoulders, blue heads, white veins, and long, thin capes made of clouds, but I was twenty and hadn't been laid in three years, so the sight of all that beauty didn't do it for me. I yawned like a baboon and crossed my legs. A skinny dude with chin stubble and curly black hair sat in front of me. I recognized him from the pizza joint at the station. He offered a hand and introduced himself as Bret from South Carolina. I took his mitt and shook it.

"Johann from North California."

He chuckled and reclined. Our train pulled away from *Åndalsnes stasjon.*[56] We got to shooting the breeze. He told me he was doing a summer abroad program in microbiology at the University of Oslo. He mentioned he had a girlfriend of two years back in Charleston.

"But therein lies the problem," he said. "See, I met this Norwegian chick who's an absolute goddess—blond hair, hazel eyes, soft skin, the works, right? I tried to resist her, but she took a liking to me right away. I even told her I had a girlfriend, and you know what her response was? 'Meet me at my cabin on Friday and we'll talk about it.' That was Wednesday. Now, here it is Monday, and I've just

---

[56] Railway station in Åndalsnes, a town on the southwestern coast of Norway.

spent three days cheatin'."

He hung his head. I glared at him under my visor.

"I know I'm supposed to feel bad for you. But I'm finding it tough."

"Haha, fair enough. Anyways, what's your deal?"

I told him I'd done a tour of Turkey with my mom; I'd left her at Frankfurt Airport and gone solo through Denmark, Sweden, and Norway. I said it had been pretty but uneventful.

"There's only so many waterfalls, fjords, and folktales you can take before your head rolls off your neck with boredom."

He laughed and asked where I was headed. I told him the same night he'd taken the train to bang his mistress, I'd been at a shitty club in Bergen,[57] nursing a ten-dollar beer and talking to some goofy Norwegian dude dressed in FUBU[58] who swore the best place to party on the cheap was Pärnu.[59] Bret asked how I could trust that.

"Well, he ended all his sentences with 'Yo.' Plus, he mentioned that his dad was a big record producer who

---

[57] City surrounded by mountains on the west coast of Norway; it is the country's second largest. According to local tradition, the city was founded in 1070 AD by King Olav Kyrre and was named Bjørgvin: "the green meadow among the mountains." It served as Norway's capital in the 13th century.

[58] American hip hop apparel company that produces casual wear, sportswear, a suit collection, eyewear, belts, and shoes. FUBU stands for "For Us, By Us," which, according to many, refers to African Americans. The acronym was created when founders Daymond John, J. Alexander Martin, Keith Perrin, and Carlton Brown were brainstorming a catchy four-letter word following other big brands such as Nike and Coke.

[59] Fourth largest city in Estonia. Located in the southwest, on the coast of Pärnu Bay, an inlet of the Gulf of Riga in the Baltic Sea. Due to its many hotels, restaurants, clubs, and beaches, Pärnu has become known as Estonia's Summer Capital. Finns, Swedes, Russians, Germans, Latvians, and Norwegians flock there for holiday. The city is also known for its seawall. According to legend, if a couple holds hands while walking along the wall and kisses at its endpoint, they will stay together forever.

worked with P. Diddy.[60] So, he had to be telling the truth."

Bret whooped. I invited him to join me. He folded his hands.

"I'd love to, bro. But I've got lab work tomorrow. As it is, I'm a day late."

I nodded solemnly; I accepted that I'd be free-ballin' it. I exchanged more travel stories with my new homie. On the outskirts of Oslo, I went to the can and took a shit. I watched in awe as my turd spiraled down and smacked the train tracks. I washed my hands and returned to my seat. Bret asked how the deed went.

"You're not gonna believe this, but—"

A commotion broke my flow. I looked ahead and saw a dude with a big, black backpack coming down the aisle. His chest was wide and his arms were ripped. He had jaw-length blond hair and skin burnt pink. His eyes were two blue comets. His grin was long and wild and fitted with bleached teeth. He walked toward us, his straps slapping against the seatbacks. His energy radiated like bomb heat. It made me smile uncontrollably—like a dirty joke had chilled on my brainstem, then jumped out at me in the middle of a quiet library. He stopped in front of us and wiped the sweat from his brow.

"Yous mind if I join ya?" he asked.

We offered a seat. We introduced ourselves and asked his deets. He said he was Johnny from New South Wales,[61]

---

[60] Sean Combs, born Sean John Combs, November 4, 1969, also known by the stage names Puff Daddy, P. Diddy, Puffy, or Diddy, is an American record producer, entrepreneur, and rapper. He founded Bad Boy Records in 1993 and has produced major artists such as The Notorious B.I.G., Mary J. Blige, and Usher.

[61] State on the east coast of Australia. It borders Queensland to the north, Victoria to the south, and South Australia to the west. The state's capital is Sydney, which is also Australia's most populous city. Coal and related products are the state's biggest exports; they account for roughly 19% of all its exports. N.S.W. has the largest population of aboriginal inhabitants in the country. Aboriginal groups include the Wodi Wodi, Bundjalung, Wiradjiri, Gamilaray, Yuin, Ngarigo, Gweagal, and Ngiyampaa peoples.

that he'd been in Trondheim[62] visiting a friend. We asked him how he liked Norway. He teetertottered his thumb and pinky.

"So-so, mates. Don't get me wrong, it's bloody gorgeous, and if you find the right girl, she'll shag ya brains out. But it's twenty Oz[63] dollars a beer, and to be honest, the clubs are shit."

We agreed with him on all counts. We asked him what his plans were. He flashed his pearlies and turned up his thumbs.

"I'm lookin' to *paaty*. Yous know where I can make that happen?"

"I'm headed to Pärnu," I said.

"What's that?"

"It's a little town on the southern coast of Estonia. Supposedly, it's *the* place to party. Plus, it's cheap."

"Aw beauty, I'm there! We all goin' tomorrow?"

Bret's face crumbled like a lump of dry seagull shit.

"I'd love to, guys, but I've got work to do. I know a place we can go tonight, though. It's not far from the station and it's got beers for under ten bucks."

"Rippa,"[64] Johnny said.

We pulled into *Oslo sentralstasjon* at nightfall. We grabbed our packs and walked to Torgatta gate.[65] We entered a bar with steel tables and birchwood walls. We ordered a round of Ringnes[66] and chatted. Johnny told us about the

---

[62] City and municipality in Trøndelag county. It had a population of 205,332 (2020), making it the third most populous municipality in Norway. The city lies on the south shore of Trondheim Fjord at the mouth of the River Nidelva. Originally founded in 997 as a trading post, Trondheim served as the capital of Norway during the Viking Age until 1217.

[63] Slang for Australia.

[64] Australian slang for fantastic or excellent.

[65] Short pedestrian street in central Oslo known for its many restaurants, cafés, and bars.

[66] Beer from the largest brewer in Norway. It was founded in 1876 by brothers Amund and Ellef Ringnes.

"friend" he'd been visiting in Trondheim. He pulled out his video camera and switched on the viewfinder.

"Here she is."

A girl in a thin blue nightgown flitted across the screen. She had wavy black hair and pale skin and long, pretty legs. Johnny play-chased her onto a king-sized bed. She giggled and threw a pillow at the lens. He laughed and the scene ended. I asked him what had happened next. He stuck his fronts over his lip and grinned.

"I rooted[67] 'ah."

I chuckled like, "Yeah, I know how it goes." He fed off it and busted out his phone. He opened a recent text from the girl.

"Hey, Johnny Bravo," he read in a shrill voice. "I miss you and wish you could come back soon. My pussy juices are waiting for you. XXX Tina."

My stomach flamed with jealousy. I guzzled the rest of my beer and ordered another. Bret took the stage and spoke of his Norwegian squeeze. This fired Johnny up and he showed more videos of Tina and told more stories of girls he'd banged. I drank and feigned savvy. It kept the spotlight off me.

Bret called it quits at midnight. He said he had enough space for one person on his floor. Johnny let me take it; he'd already booked a hostel. I shook his hand and thanked him. We planned to meet at the station the next morning at eight. Bret and I took a cab to his uni. His dorm was smaller than a tin of Viennese weenies. I cleared a space on the carpet of beer cans and dirty underwear. I unfurled the ugly blue-and-yellow sleeping bag I'd bought in Turkey. Bret clicked off the lights and said goodnight. I lay down, pulled my visor over my eyes, and crashed.

---

[67] Australian slang meaning fuck or screw.

I woke up to the sun burning my scalp. I packed my shit, thanked Bret, and cut. I took a thousand-dollar cab to the station. I arrived at eight and bought a cheese Danish. Johnny rolled up forty minutes later. We asked the ticket lady about the morning train to Stockholm. She said it was sold out. We got two spots on the five o'clock. Neither of us had seen the city. We locked our bags and split.

We hit the wharf and saw a photo exhibition. We did a mini cruise around *Oslofjord* [68] and ogled the cute tour guide. We got Cokes and hit Vigeland Park.[69] It was cool, but there were too many granite-hewn dudes with their dicks dangling. One statue stood out; it was a pinnacle of naked people woven together. I saw asses and cocks and balls and pussies. They belonged to grownups and babies and rickety old men and ladies. Johnny eyed the thing and sniffed.

"Looks like an orgy-pop."[70]

We laughed and sat on the grass. What Vigeland lacked in appealing artwork it made up for in ass. Beautiful Nordic women with platinum hair and bronze skin wandered the lanes. Johnny and I soaked them in and clinked bottles. We chopped it up for a couple hours. Besides travel and chicks, I found out we had a lot in

---

[68] Inlet in southeast Norway, stretching down to Langesund in the south to Oslo in the north. On its eastern and western shores, three of the best-preserved Viking ships were unearthed. Norwegian painter Edvard Munch had a cottage and studio on the fjord. It appears in several of his paintings, including *Girls on the Pier* and *The Scream.*

[69] Public park located in the West End borough of Frogner in Oslo. The park contains the Vigeland installation, a permanent sculpture, bridge, and fountain collection created by Gustav Vigeland between 1924 and 1943. The installation is sometimes called Vigeland Park, though, this is considered the "tourist name." Oslo natives call it Frogner Park.

[70] Johnny coined this phrase, which I took to mean, "An orgy in the shape of a giant popsicle." He was referring to a 17-meter sculpture called The Monolith at (ahem) Frogner Park. The sculpture is carved out of a single stone block—hence the name—and depicts 121 men, women, and children of different ages, all woven together in a beautiful, yet gruesome tower. Many interpret the sculpture as a symbol of resurrection and man's longing for spirituality . . . or orgies.

common. We both ate fast and had ADHD.[71] We both spoke our minds, wrote crooked, and made friends quickly. We even shared the joy of having local argots. I spit him some ROAST,[72] and he talked a bit of slang from his hometown Singleton.[73] I asked him what he did there. He tore out a handful of grass.

"Aww, fuck-all, mate," he said, tossing it. "It's just a little mining town. I dig coal six months outta the year. It's bloody dangerous but it pays heaps. I save most of what I make. The other six months, I travel."

"Damn, how many countries you been to?"

"Seventy-five. But I wanna do a hundred before I'm thirty."

"How old are you now?"

"Twenty-nine."

"Christ, I'm already twenty and I've only been to thirty."

"You still got time, mate."

"Yeah, maybe when it comes to countries."

"Whaddaya mean?"

"Now that we're traveling together, I might as well tell you."

---

[71] Attention deficit hyperactivity disorder (ADHD) is a behavioral and neurodevelopmental disorder characterized by attention deficit, hyperactivity, disruptiveness, and impulsivity, which are pervasive, impairing, and otherwise age inappropriate. Causes are attributed to genetic factors such as reduced dopamine levels in the brain, and environmental factors such as low birth weight, premature delivery, and alcohol, tobacco, or drug use during pregnancy. The usual onset is before the age of six. According to certain criteria, the condition affects 5-7% of children and 2-5% of adults.

[72] Dialect of English my friends and I created. The acronym stands for Result of a Small Town. The town in reference is Livermore, California, where we all grew up.

[73] Town of 16,346 on the banks of the Hunter River in New South Wales, Australia. It is 144 km (89 mi) north-north-west of Sydney, and 70 km (43 mi) north-west of Newcastle. The traditional custodians of the land around what is now Singleton (established c.a. 1820) are the Wonnarua, who have occupied the Upper Hunter Valley for over 30,000 years. The town's largest industry is coal mining, which employs 24% of its workforce.

"You got a one-inch wanka?"

"Haha, nope. But I have only been with one chick."

I told him the story of my high school girlfriend, how we'd been each other's first and screwed a handful of times. We'd broken up in June of '99.

"And here it is July of '02 and I still haven't been laid."

"Why the hell not?"

"Because," I said, adjusting my visor. "I started losing my hair and it made me insecure."

He swiped the air.

"Oh bollocks. You're a good-lookin' bloke. These sheilas would be lucky to have you shag 'em."

"Really?"

"Of course, mate. Stick with me. By the time we finish with Pärnu, you'll be beatin' 'em off with a stick."

We took a cab to the station and boarded our train. It left at 5:00 p.m. on the dot. The ride was long and boring. Johnny livened it by showing me videos of him running with the bulls in Spain. We arrived in Stockholm at ten-thirty. We hit the streets and searched for a hostel. The first few we checked were booked. We wandered in circles for two hours. We finally found a joint that had vacancies. It was cramped, dingy, and run by a fat dude with a skullet[74] and a scraggly beard. He charged us twenty-five bucks a head for a standard double. I was fit to wring his neck, but he tossed in a free breakfast. We paid the old

---

[74] Extreme form of the mullet hairstyle, in which the hair at the back of the head is kept long, while the hair on the top and at the sides is buzzed, shaved to the skin, or simply missing due to male pattern baldness. Sources claim that the skullet was originally a hairstyle from ancient East Asia used to accentuate the head—a symbol of wisdom. The mullet itself was possibly worn by natives of ancient Britain, young males in early Byzantium, and certain tribes of Native Americans. In his booklet, *Mourt's Relation*, which documents the landing of The Mayflower and the settling of the Plymouth Colony, author Edward Winslow describes the Plymouth pilgrims' first encounter with the Samoset (chief) of the Abenaki tribe in 1621: "He was a tall straight man, the hair of his head black, long behind, only short before, none on his face at all."

fucker and dumped our shit. I wanted to crash, but Johnny swore that his best mate said Stockholm, despite being pricy, was "a real piss-up." I wasn't sure what he meant. I assumed he was referring to the ready availability of drinks and/or pussy. I groaned and threw on a shirt. I spritzed Axe on my pits and scrubbed my visor. Johnny asked why I wore the thing at night. I told him my hairline didn't stop receding when the sun went down.

We made it out by 1:00 a.m. The streets were empty except for a few old drunks folding themselves at bus stops. Johnny was excited just the same. He was like a cocker spaniel with a centrifuge that powered his balls, muscles, guts, and brains. He clapped and spun and pointed at things of interest. I tried to keep up with him, but I couldn't garner the oomph. He soon noticed my downer mood. He stopped and asked what the problem was. I dragged my shoe-tip across the sidewalk.

"I'm nervous."

"About what?"

"Talking to chicks."

"Why?"

"Because I don't know what to say."

"Aw, that's the beauty part. None'a these chicks know ya from Bob, so you can tell 'em any bloody thing ya want."

"Really?"

"Shit yeah! You think I'm gonna tell 'em I'm a coal miner from woop woop, N.S.W.? Fuck no, mate. As far as they're concerned, I'm a crocodile 'resla from the dodgiest part of Oz."

"Then what the fuck am I?"

"You're an oil billionaire from Cali*foooo*rnia, *maaaan*," he said, mimicking my accent.

"Alright. But if this goes south, it's on you."

We found an open bar at the edge of town. They charged ten bucks at the door and made me remove my visor. This put a urine squirt in my *Vichyssoise*.[75] Johnny tried to lift my spirits by getting me a Red Bull and vodka. He ordered himself a Tokyo Tea.[76] We sat at a table near the dancefloor. A few cute girls were shimmying in a circle. We sipped our drinks and planned our next move. Two dudes with shaggy manes and goatees took the seats across from us. They said hello and asked where we were from.

We told them "Oz and Cali" and asked them the same. They said they were from Kurdistan[77] but they lived in Stockholm. I asked how they liked it.

"It's perfect," they said. "Scandinavian women will fuck anyone."

Johnny raised his eyebrows.

"Then what are yous doin' here yabberin' to us?"

The shorter Kurd sniggered.

"How old are you?" he asked Johnny.

"Twenty-nine."

"Yeah? Well, you look like thirty-seven."

Johnny nodded and swallowed his drink. He stood,

---

[75] Thick French soup made of boiled and puréed leeks, onions, potatoes, cream, and chicken stock. It is traditionally served cold, but it can be eaten hot. The origins of the soup are debated; one version of the story is that Louis XV of France was afraid of being poisoned and had so many servant-tasters, that by the time he felt it was safe to eat, the soup was cold; since he enjoyed it that way, it became a cold soup.

[76] Spin on the Long Island Iced Tea made with vodka, tequila, white rum, gin, Cointreau, fresh lemon juice, simple syrup, soda water, and the honeydew melon flavored liqueur Midori, which gives the drink its brilliant green color.

[77] Kurdistan (lit. Land of the Kurds) is a roughly defined geo-cultural territory in Western Asia wherein ethnic Kurds form a prominent majority, and where their culture, languages, and national identity have historically been based. Geographically, Kurdistan generally comprises the following four areas: southeastern Turkey (Northern Kurdistan), northern Iraq (Southern Kurdistan), north-western Iran (Eastern Kurdistan), and northern Syria (Western Kurdistan). The Kurdish languages constitute a dialect continuum belonging to the Iranian branch of the Indo-European language family. The three main Kurdish languages are Northern Kurdish (Kurmanji), Central Kurdish (Sorani), and Southern Kurdish (Xwarîn). Most Kurds (~15 million people) speak Kurmanji.

fixed his hair, and walked onto the dancefloor. He approached the hottest girl in the circle. She was tall and blond, with a caramel body wrapped in a strapless dress. He said something in her ear that made her laugh. She put her arms around his shoulders, and they danced for three songs. They made out at the end. Johnny strutted back to the table with her number on a napkin. He tossed it in the Kurds' faces.

"Howzat for thirty-seven?" he said.

The Kurds snarled and left. My jaw hit my lap.

We woke up hungover at noon. We guzzled water, did pushups, and took showers. I bic'd[78] my head while Johnny went down for breakfast. I joined him twenty minutes later with a shiny, bald scalp. He greeted me with a smile. I saw that he'd eaten everything except two bites of ham and a slice of bread. He stared at them like a dog waiting for its owner's command.

"Go ahead, mate," I said. "You deserve it for last night's performance."

He grabbed the food and scarfed it. I drank a glass of OJ, then we packed our bags and split. We walked to the train station and bought tickets for the overnight Viking Line[79] to Helsinki. It didn't depart until evening. We left and walked to the center. I bought souvenirs while Johnny folded his arms and kicked around a plastic bag. We walked back to the station. We took a bus to the docks and peeped our ship. It was ten stories high and three football fields long. It looked like a floating megamall. We took photos and got on. The woman closed the gate behind us. We asked her the dilly. She said we were the last to board.

We laughed at our luck. We lugged our shit to the

---

[78] NorCal slang meaning shaved with a Bic razor.

[79] Finnish shipping company that operates a fleet of ferries and cruise-ferries between Finland, Sweden, and Estonia.

common room on the tenth floor. It was filled with backpackers who'd spread out their sleeping bags in a filthy mosaic. We picked a spot in the dung heap and pitched camp. We stashed our valuables in a locker and scoped the scene. We saw a bar, a restaurant, and a grocery store. We hit the bar first. We ordered a pair of eight-dollar beers. Sat across the stools were three Irish dudes; we'd met them on our hostel hunt the night before. Conor was tall and skinny with freckles and red hair. David was short and stalky with dimples and black hair. Pat was midsized with a potbelly and an overbite. He had brown hair, brown eyes, and an accent so thick you could use it to hang wallpaper.

We chatted with them for a bit, then hit the grocery store. We bought cider, beer, and whiskey, then we all went to the common room. We popped bottles and drank. The cider and beer were warm, and the whiskey tasted like ass. We finished half our stash and hit the restaurant. We ordered a feast of pig knuckle and trout and three kinds of pasta. We wolfed our food and went back to the booze. People were passed out in their sleeping bags, but we still drained liquor and laughed.

We mobbed the disco at midnight. A band was playing, and the dancefloor was packed. We got drinks and grabbed a table. Johnny, Conor, and David busted a move. Pat and I sat back and watched. Johnny knew what he was doing but the others were clueless. Conor did The Robot[80] and David did The Shopping Cart.[81] They looked like two retards trying to make it to the bathroom before they shat themselves. Pat and I had a good chuckle. I

---

[80] Street dance style comprised of robot-like movements, which are started and finished with a "dimestop" (a very abrupt stop), to give the impression of motors starting and stopping.

[81] Dance style in which the performer pretends they are shopping at a supermarket by grabbing imaginary items from imaginary shelves and throwing them into an imaginary shopping cart while they trot across the dancefloor.

couldn't understand the motherfucker, but it didn't matter.

The guys came back to the table an hour later. Conor and David were spent, but Johnny still wanted to raise hell. We spotted a table of blondes yuckin' it up. Johnny thought they were Swedes, but I said they were Finns.

"How do you know?" he asked.

"Because Finnish sounds like 'Peepee-poopoo-kaka' over and over again."

The table roared with laughter. Johnny stood and jabbed his thumb.

"You're on, mate."

My stomach turned to soup.

"What the hell do I say to them?"

"Haha. Just tell 'em what you told me."

I groaned and stood. I straightened my shirt and led the way. I thought desperately about what to say. I knew I couldn't tell these chicks their language sounded like an infant cooing in a pool of its excrement. I remembered a phrase in Finnish I'd learned from Encarta.[82] I repeated it a few times under my breath. I fixed my visor and approached the table. I tapped the nearest girl.

"Excuse me. Are you Finnish?"

"Yes," she replied.

"Well . . . *Parempi pyy pivossa kuin kaksi oksalla.*"

She raised her brow and upper lip. She turned and continued chatting. Johnny took me to one side.

"What the hell did you say to her?" he asked.

I dimpled the corners of my mouth.

"I'm pretty sure I said, 'A bird in the hand is worth two in the bush.'"

"Why the fuck would you go and say a thing like that?"

---

[82] Digital multimedia encyclopedia published by Microsoft from 1993 to 2009. Originally sold on CD-ROM or DVD, it was also available on the internet via an annual subscription. Encarta consisted of articles, photos, illustrations, music clips, videos, interactive content, timelines, maps, atlases, homework tools, and soundbites in dozens of languages. It was the Wikipedia for kids in the 90s.

"It's all I know in Finnish."

"Mate, if you're gonna speak to a woman in her language, you learn, 'Your eyes are pretty,' or, 'I like your smile.' Not some shit that sounds like you floppin' your wanka on her palm will get her off as much as the rootin' she just got from two blokes."

I grinned sheepishly. Johnny coughed out a laugh.

"Why don't we try the dancefloor."

"But I can't dance."

"Watch what I do for a bit, then do the same."

"Alright."

I followed him out. He clapped his hands and slipped into the crowd. I stood at the periphery and watched. He pointed his toes and swirled his legs and danced circles around the ladies. I knew I didn't have a Chinaman's chance at pulling that off. I opted for a wiggle of the bum and a quick two-step. It didn't earn me a shower of panties, but I got a couple looks. This was enough to encourage me to ask some girls to dance. They turned me down, of course. But at least I knew that somewhere in my scrotum a measly pair of balls did lie.

I went back to the table and chilled. Conor and David were off cuttin' a rug again, and Pat was at another table making out with a middle-aged Swedish woman who looked like a dude. I ordered a beer and watched the shenanigans. The band played a few more songs and Johnny charmed a few more ladies and Conor and David about had themselves a schizoid embolism. Pat took off with Nick Nolte.[83] The music crescendoed and the band said *adieux*.

Johnny came back all sweat and hair and smiles. He

---

[83] American actor, producer, author, and former jeans model, was born February 8, 1941, in Omaha, Nebraska—my favorite state. He won the Golden Globe Award for Best Actor and was nominated for the Academy Award for Best Actor for the 1991 film *The Prince of Tides*. He received Academy Award nominations for *Affliction* (1998) and *Warrior* (2011). He is known for his "bad-boy reputation" due to his history of alcoholism and substance abuse.

plopped in his chair and guzzled the last of his brew. Conor and David said goodnight and split. We thought about bouncing too. We scanned the area. The lead singer was sitting alone. She was tall and thin and pretty. She had blue eyes, brown hair, and tan skin. Johnny turned and grinned.

"We're gonna go over there. And you're gonna do the talkin'. Only this time you're gonna start with, 'Hey, my name is Johann,' and not some bollocks that a bloody elf in a fairytale would say, alright?"

"Alright."

We got new beers and walked to the singer's table. Johnny broke the ice and handed me the mic. I said exactly what he told me. She looked confused, but she didn't turn away. She said hello, and that her name was Kirsty. I said I was pleased to meet her and asked if we could sit. She upturned her hand.

"I don't own these chairs," she said.

We took that as a "Yes." We sat and sipped our beers and chatted. She was quiet at first. After a while, she shared that she was twenty-one, from Sweden, and had been singing since she was a kid. We asked what her plans were. She thinned her eyes.

"My guitarist, Paul, and I will drink beers in my room in twenty minutes. You can join if you are good boys."

We smiled so hard our cheeks hurt. We finished our beers and grabbed more booze at the all-night grocery store. Johnny got his camera, and we followed Kirsty to her room. It was eighteen-by-nine with a table, two bunk beds, and a dinky shitter. We sat at the table and cracked our beers. Paul came, guitar-in-hand, a few minutes later. He wore a leopard-print T-shirt and a white beanie. He had black hair, black eyes, and a flavor-saver[84] in the shape of

---

[84] Tuft of facial hair beneath the lower lip that presumably saves the flavor of whatever its owner eats. This term is usually used with reference to eating pussy.

a spade. He sat with us and drank. We chatted about music, and after a little coaxing, we got Kirsty to sing. Her voice was rich and beautiful. It evoked images of crystals being melted under flame. Paul accompanied her with his guitar. Johnny and I joined, and we sang and sang.

The sun peaked through the blinds at 4:00 a.m. We finished our beers and called it. Kirsty and Paul offered us their extra bunks. This meant one of us would stay and the other would go. I looked at Johnny with puppy dog eyes. He patted me on the shoulder.

"Why don't I take Paul's bunk, mate. I'm knackered."

I thanked him quietly. He said no worries and left. I was alone with Kirsty. I started to feel giddy. My excitement was immediately drowned by fear; I was a naked child surrounded by a thousand masturbating maniacs. I suppressed the image and steadied my countenance. I told Kirsty I'd be back in a minute. I went to the men's room and puked in the sink. I washed my face twelve times then looked in the mirror. I saw the face of a diseased man. I slapped it and washed it again. I dried myself with paper towels and went to the common room. I grabbed my toiletries and a clean pair of boxers and returned to Kirsty's. I knocked on her door three times. She opened it wearing a violet negligee. I almost threw a blood clot. I scratched my neck and entered. She closed the door behind me. We stood in the blueness of dawn. She looked at my visor. She reached up and pulled it from my scalp. I felt like a devil in an angel's suit having his halo removed. She placed my visor on the table and looked at me.

"Why do you wear that thing?"

"Because I'm losing my hair, and it makes me feel ugly."

She lifted her hand and ran her fingers down my cheek.

"But your face is so beautiful."

The storm in my head froze. I leaned forward to kiss

her. Something dislodged. The clouds swallowed my eyes. I turned and climbed onto the top bunk.

"Goodnight, Kirsty."

"Goodnight, Johann."

I woke up at ten to people talking. I pretended I was still asleep. I heard Johnny ask Kirsty what had happened between us. She said, "I have to know a person before I sleep with them." Johnny said that was cool. I yawned and stretched my arms. I jumped from my bunk and popped on my visor. My friends laughed. We chatted about sex. I mirrored Kirsty's sentiment. Her expression told me she knew I'd been listening. I didn't care.

Our boat docked in Helsinki at noon. We got off and explored. We saw white marble buildings and green parks, a mint-domed cathedral,[85] and loads of cafés. It was a pretty town but not very exciting. We decided to take the ferry to Tallinn[86] that day. We asked Paul and Kirsty if

---

[85] Helsinki Cathedral – a Finnish Evangelical Lutheran cathedral located in the neighborhood of Kruununhaka (say that ten times fast) in the center of Helsinki at Senate Square. It was built from 1830–1852 as a tribute to Tsar Nicholas I of Russia. With its five mint-colored domes topped with golden crosses, it is the most distinct landmark in Helsinki, and possibly the most famous structure in Finland. The opening sequence of the music video for "Sandstorm" by Finnish DJ and record producer Darude was filmed on Senate Square, prominently featuring the cathedral in the background.

[86] The most populous and capital city of Estonia, with 444,532 people (2021). It is situated in northern Estonia, on the Gulf of Finland, which is part of the Baltic Sea. Its name is derived from the Estonian, "*Taani-linn*," meaning 'Danish-town,' after the Danes built a castle in place of the Estonian stronghold at Lindanisse – capital of the ancient Estonian country of Revala. From the 13th century until the first half of the 20th century, Tallinn was known by variants of its other historical name "Reval" derived from the name of said country. The city's most prominent landmark is St. Olaf's Church, which at approximately 120m (almost 400 feet) was reportedly the tallest building in the world from 1549 to 1625.

they'd join us. They said they couldn't as they had a show to do on the boat that night. I felt a terrible pain in my chest. I knew this was the last time I'd see Kirsty. I asked Johnny to snap a photo of us. We stood on the sidewalk with the cathedral in the background. Kirsty was wearing a black bowler hat. I flattered myself in thinking she'd worn it for me. I put my arm around her and smiled. She did the same and the camera clicked. We exchanged emails and addresses. I told her if she was ever in Cali, she could stay with me. She told me the same about Stockholm. For a second, I thought about leaving with her. Then I remembered Johnny and our mission to Pärnu. It was enough to stop me.

We said goodbye and went to the docks. We caught the next express ferry, which left at five o'clock. Johnny slept the whole way. I chatted with a Russian boy named Sergei, who was deep into trance music. He gifted me a CD with a purple skull embossed on the front. It made me feel a tad better.

We pulled into Tallinn at seven. I nudged Johnny awake and we bounced. We walked from the ferry station toward Old Town. We entered under a stone archway. It revealed a beautiful sight: redbrick roofs, black iron church spires, pastel facades, and clocktowers crawling with ivy. The roads were made of blue cobblestone. The Squares were bustling and lined with cafés. We found a little Indian restaurant on *Raekoja plats*.[87] We ordered curries and beers and mused at Tallinn Town Hall.[88]

---

[87] Town square beside Tallinn Town Hall in the center of Tallinn's Old Town. Numerous festivals and concerts are held there, and several bars and restaurants are located nearby. The square also hosts a market, with stalls selling traditional Estonian arts and crafts.

[88] Oldest town hall in the Baltics and Scandinavia. The height of its tower is 64m (210 feet). The vane "Old Thomas" on the top of the tower has become one of the symbols of Tallinn. The first vane depicting Old Thomas was placed on the tower's peak in 1530. According to legend, the model for the vane was a peasant named Thomas who, as a young boy, became famous for winning a crossbow competition held by the

Johnny wanted to rip shit up. I was game but still depressed.

We finished our food and found a hostel. We hit a bar and drank till the lights blurred and the streets became a maze. We stumbled around searching for a spot to party. We came across a club called Krush. It had marble columns, stone steps, vaulted ceilings, and neon windows. We heard the feverish beat of trance music. We paid the doorman and walked inside. We saw brass poles, DJ booths, opera balconies, and ladies in cages. The dancefloor was flooded with ravers. The main stage was lit, and the wall screen was flashing colors. We got a table and ordered drinks. Johnny sucked his down and went to dance. I tried to get up, but I couldn't. I slouched in my seat and tongued my straw. An apelike bouncer smacked a drunk in the face; he spit blood on the wall and collapsed, and with him went the night.

I woke up with a splitting hangover. I heard Johnny singing in the shower. I grabbed my water and chugged it. I sat up and puked in the trashcan. Johnny walked outta the bathroom with a towel around his waist. The steam followed him like a jazzy ghost. He slipped on his boxers and clapped his hands.

"You ready to destroy Pärnu?"

Baltic German elite. The competition involved shooting down a colorful wooden parrot placed on the top of a post. Thomas was the only one to shoot it down. As his status did not actually allow him to compete, he did not get the prize. Instead, thanks to the mayor, he received the honor of being a city guard, and was immortalized by the vane. Thomas's vane stayed on guard until March 1944 when the tower burst into flames during a series of air raids by the German Luftwaffe and Soviet Long Range Aviation. The raids destroyed 8,000 buildings, approximately a third of the city. In 1952, the tower was restored, and a copy of Old Thomas was installed. In 1996, the vane was again replaced, as the one from 1952 was in bad condition. The original Old Thomas from 1530, is now in the basement of Tallinn Town Hall.

I held my forehead and moaned.

"I guess."

I got up and took a scalding shower. I bic'd my head and brushed my teeth and packed my bag. I dressed in the same outfit. Johnny scolded me, but I didn't give a crap. We walked to the bus station. We boarded the three o'clock and took our seats. Johnny passed out. I listened to music and studied Estonian.[89] I learned the numbers and a few key phrases; nothing to blow anyone's mind, but enough to get me in the door.

We arrived at five past five. We walked through downtown and found a hostel on *Pärnu rand*.[90] We dropped our bags and went to dinner. We ate at an Estonian place in the center. We ordered smoked pork hock and potato salad, blood dumplings and meat jelly, and sandwiches made of sprat.[91] We munched our food and eyed our surroundings. The buildings were pink and orange and green with flower-troughed windows and black steeples. The ladies threading around them could give a man a heart attack. They had long, creamy legs and strawberry blond hair and eyes so blue they made saxophones croon.

We finished dinner and hit the beach. We walked along the sand till we came to a club called Sundance. It had two floors and a big balcony. Rock music was shaking the windows. We stopped at the entrance. We flipped the doorman a nickel and went inside. The dancefloor was the

---

[89] Estonian belongs to the Finnic branch of the Uralic language family. It is the official language of Estonia, spoken natively by about 1.1 million people. It is the second-most-spoken language among the Finnic languages—Finnish being the first. Alongside Finnish, Hungarian, and Maltese, Estonian is one of the four official languages of the European Union that is not of Indo-European origin.

[90] Beach on Pärnu Bay, administratively in Pärnu, Estonia. In the summer, it is a mecca for sunbathers and swimmers, primarily from Scandinavia, the Baltic States, and Russia.

[91] Common name applied to a group of forage fish. In Estonia, they are the main ingredient in the *kiluvõileib*, which is an open-faced sandwich consisting of a slice of rye bread that is topped with a marinated sprat fillet.

size of a jet hangar. Giant disco balls hung from the ceiling and a mob of sweaty Scandinavians throbbed underneath. We pushed our way to the bar. We ordered two beers each and went to the balcony. We sipped our drinks and scanned. We spotted a lone blonde at the railing. Johnny nudged me with his elbow.

"Go talk to her, mate."

I downed one beer and gulped the other.

"Alright."

I walked over and stood next to her. She smelled like a sprig of jasmine. I waited till she noticed me. I smiled and asked her name. She said it was Juuli. I told her mine was Johann. We bonded on the "J." We spit a few more pleasantries. I grew a pair of testis. I touched her hand and gazed at her.

"*Su silmad on ilusad,*" I said.

Her irises lit up like Ferris wheels. She grinned and bounced and clapped her hands. I silently thanked Johnny. I had it in the bag. I moved in for the kiss. A hand grabbed my shirt. Another stabbed a finger at my chest.

"Don't touch her," a voice yelled.

I looked up and saw a dude staring back at me. He was tall and muscly and dressed in black. He had a blond flattop and the face of a bulldog. A silver cross hung from a cable chain around his neck. He seized Juuli by the wrist and yanked her inside. She simpered and waved goodbye. I waved back and dropped my chin. Johnny came and put his arm around me.

"No worries, mate," he said, handing me a fresh beer. "You'll get 'em next time."

I swigged it and got another. We took shots and moved onto car bombs. I blacked out for three hours. I came to as we were walking on the beach with some dude who was also named Johann. He and Johnny had MILFs on their arms. I was alone and that seemed fitting. The ladies talked about going back to their place. I was shitfaced and in no mood for games. I tipped everyone two and split. I heard Johann yell something at me and laugh. I ignored him and stumbled to the hostel. I stripped to my skivvies, washed my face, and crashed.

I woke up in the late afternoon. Johnny was sprawled on his bed. I asked him how it went. He rubbed his eyes and sniffed.

"Beauty. We snorted coke and shagged all morning."

"Congratulations. I suppose you'll wanna sleep all day?"

"Nah. Gonna meet Johann number two and his mates on the beach for beers."

"Have fun."

"Oh no, ya don't."

"What?"

"I'm not gonna let ya stay here 'n wank[92] in the dunny.[93] You're comin' with."

"Why?"

"'Cuz this is our trip, mate."

I huffed and got outta bed. I put on my shorts and thongs and donned my visor. Johnny grabbed his towel and slipped on his shades.

"And no whingin'."[94]

"Whatever that means."

We walked to the beach and met my namesake. He was chilling faceup on a white towel. I remembered vaguely that he'd been hirsute. Seeing him now made me think of Teen Wolf.[95] Hair covered his chest, stomach, and legs. It sprouted from his toes and fingers and curled from

---

[92] Australian slang meaning masturbate or jerk off.

[93] Australian slang for toilet or crapper.

[94] Australian slang meaning whine or complain.

[95] 1985 American fantasy comedy directed by Rod Daniel. Michael J. Fox stars as the main character, a high school student whose average life is changed when he discovers that he is a werewolf.

his neck and shoulders. He had a beard like a cave hermit and earlocks for dayz.[96] The only place he didn't have hair was the top of his head. I unfurled my towel and sat.

"How's the tanning?" I asked.

"Perfect," he said, turning over. "How was home alone?"

"Haven't seen it in years."

"What?"

"Never mind."

I noticed Sasquatch had a friend. He was short and skinny with a fuzzy blond head. He raised his hand and waved.

"Hi, I am Ralf," he said, with the voice of a friendly robot.

Johnny and I introduced ourselves. We chatted with Ralf while Cousin Itt[97] sunned his dingleberries. Ralf mentioned he had a cabin outside of Tallinn. He asked if we had plans after Pärnu. We told him we hadn't.

"It is settled then," he said. "You guys will stay wif me."

We accepted the invitation. We celebrated by cracking beers. We sipped them and admired the beach. A shadow obstructed our view. I looked up to find its source. He was tall and ripped and slathered in tanning oil. His face was pinched and gnarly. A silver crucifix hung from his neck. I thought of grabbing a rock. He grinned and sat next to me.

"Sorry for last night," he said. "I was drunk and thought you steal my woman."

I forced a smile.

"No worries. Name's Johann."

"I'm Marko," he said, slapping my thigh. "My girlfriend go back to Tallinn so we have guy party tonight. I will find

---

[96] A long time.

[97] Hirsute fictional character in *The Addams Family* television and film series. He is short and composed entirely of floor-length blonde hair. He has an IQ of 320, and often sports a bowler hat and round sunglasses. He speaks in a warbly gibberish that is understood only by his family.

you replacement girl."

"Sounds like a plan."

Johnny and I went back to our room at sundown. We napped, showered, shaved, and ate a quick dinner. We met the guys at a club in town. Marko had reserved a booth with bottle service. He had girls waiting. The prettiest two were for him and Sweetums[98] of course. Johnny and Ralf took the next best looking. I got stuck with a frumpy Brunette. She was frowning and staring at her thumbs. I tried to cheer her up with some chitchat and a little Estonian. Marko noticed I was having trouble. He downed a shot of Viru Valge[99] and stood.

"Don't talk to them," he said. "Take them and rape them, like this!"

He grabbed his girl and pulled her onto the dancefloor. He spun her around and slammed his crotch to her ass. He looked at me and winked. I rolled my eyes and sipped my drink. The brunette looked frightened. It twisted my stomach in knots. I put money on the table and grabbed my coat. I left without saying goodbye.

We woke up at noon and checked out. We went to the street and sat on the curb. Johann and Ralf pulled up in a blue Fiat. We climbed in back with our bags and sped away. It was a dreary, overcast day. Rain sprinkled the windshield and blackened the road. We listened to hip hop

---

[98] Minor character in *The Muppets*—an ensemble group of comedic puppet characters originally created by Jim Henson. Sweetums is a nine-foot-tall ogre with thick, light-brown hair all over his body, and a large lower jaw, which juts out, revealing two tusk-like teeth. He has bushy eyebrows over round yellow eyes, a bulbous orange nose, and wears a shabby brown shirt. Despite his intimidating appearance, he is often depicted as friendly and harmless, hence his name, Sweetums.

[99] Premium, grain-based Estonian vodka. Produced by Liviko since 1962, it is the oldest vodka brand in Estonia.

and sang along; everyone except Johann, who was grooming his chest hair with a fork.

We arrived in Tallinn at two. We dropped Johann II off at his cave, then drove to the outskirts. We entered a residential neighborhood. It was pretty and green and full of trees. We parked in front of a two-story, gray-brick house with stone walls. We exited and grabbed our bags. Ralf opened the gate. An enormous mastiff jumped out. He pawed Ralf and licked his face. Ralf laughed then snapped his finger. He gave the dog a sharp command in Estonian. The dog climbed down and sat. I looked on in bewilderment.

"Your dog understands Estonian?" I asked.

Ralf knitted his brow.

"Of course."

"Wow, that's amazing."

"It is not. A dog that understands fucking Chinese is amazing."

We cracked up. The dog looked confused. We took him inside and unloaded our shit. Ralf gave us the second floor. It had a guestroom, a storeroom, and a full bath. We took showers and chilled. We ordered a pepperoni pizza and drank beers. We asked Ralf what the plan was. He said he'd spoken with Johann earlier.

"Tomorrow we'll take his boat to Saaremaa,"[100] he said.

"The island?" I asked.

"Yes. And it will be big day so you should get good sleep."

"Why? Is Johann gonna have us braid his back hair

---

[100] Largest island in Estonia, measuring 2,673 km² (1,032 sq mi), and with a population of 31,435 (2020). The island is noted for nine small meteorite craters collectively called *Kaali*. The largest of the craters measures 110 m (360 ft) in diameter and contains a small lake, known as *Kaali järv* (Lake Kaali). It was estimated that the energy of the biggest crater's impact was comparable with that of the Hiroshima bomb. The commonly accepted age estimate of the craters is 4000 ± 1000 BCE. According to archaeological finds, the territory of Saaremaa has been inhabited from at least 5000 BCE, which means the island's original inhabitants probably bore witness to the impacts.

on the beach?"

"Haha. No. But there will be big surprise."

"Oh boy."

We got up at 9:00 a.m. and drove to the docks. Ralf pointed out the boat. It had a wide deck and a cabin underneath. Johann was prepping the sail. He wore gray Adidas pants and a matching hoodie. He looked like a Georgian monk turned track star. I tried my damnedest not to laugh. We boarded and helped him. I asked what the big surprise was.

"You find out soon," he said, chuckling.

I smiled and nodded. I continued prepping the sail. I heard a stirring underneath. The cabin door opened, and a woman stepped out. She was tall and svelte and pale. She wore a peach tank top and white pants. Her hair was blond with black roots; it was pulled into a tight bun. Her face was a perfect teardrop. She had a button nose, glossy lips, and eyes so green they could be set in wedding rings. She smiled with porcelain teeth. I found it hard to breathe. Johann introduced us.

"Maarja, meet . . . *me*."

She looked confused. I rolled my eyes and extended my hand.

"I'm Johann too."

"Johann *number* two," Chewbacca corrected.

"Whatever."

"Two Johanns," Maarja said, clapping. "This will be fun."

She grabbed a beer and cracked it. Johann leaned into my ear.

"Don't say I never do nothing for you," he whispered.

We untied the boat and pushed off. We moved into the steely water at an even pace. The sky was overcast and gray. It sprinkled a tad. We drank beers and chatted. I was eager to show Maarja my Estonian. I waited for my chance. People blabbed and blabbed. Johann finished his beer. He asked Maarja for another as she was near the cooler. She opened it and looked at him.

"How many?" she asked. *"Üks? Kaks?"*

"Kolm?" I said.

She dropped the beer in her hand. She turned and faced me.

"Can you count to ten?"

"I think so."

I said the numbers slowly. I got to ten and grinned. Her eyes widened. I was locked in a tractor beam of green. It pulled me from my seat. It dragged me over the deck with my tongue out, and up to her feet. I was about to kiss them. Johann stood and yanked in the sail.

"Save it, Casanova. We are here."

I came out of my daze. Maarja said we'd resume our convo on the way back. I said okay and helped Johann. We tied down the boat and explored. Saaremaa was small but pretty; it had windmills and wheat fields, white-stone castles, and meteorite craters. Its beaches were long and yellow. Its lighthouses were of all shapes and colors, and its forest was deep and rich and green. We left the beaten path and wandered into its belly. We found an abandoned house with busted windows and a rusty roof. We pushed open the creaky door and went inside. We saw a wood-burning stove, an old bed, and a desk fraught with wood rot. Mosquitos swarmed my head. I swatted them off, but not before they scored a few good bites. My scalp swelled with knots; they rose above my visor like little teapots. I scratched them and cursed the universe. My friends slapped their knees and laughed. Maarja was to the point of tears. She put her hand on my shoulder and wiped her eyes.

"Oh, Johann," she said, gasping. "You make me laughing so much."

I almost corrected her English. I bit my tongue and made a rictus. I grabbed my itch cream and spread it on my bites. We explored a bit more then went back to the boat. We set sail and cut. Maarja and I got beers and went down into the cabin. She told me how funny I was again. I nodded and changed the subject. I asked her if she spoke any other languages. She said, "Finnish and a bit of French." I smiled and sipped my beer.

"Tes yeux sont de la plus belle nuance de vert," I said.

She smiled coyly.

"Merci beaucoup."

We chatted for an hour in French. I figured I was in like Flynn.[101] I asked if she would go out with me. She crossed her legs and touched her chin.

"On one condition," she said.

"What's that?"

"I tell you tonight."

She wrote her number on a slip of paper. She handed it to me and said we were all to meet at a bar called Loku at eight. I told her I'd be there, f'sheez. We got off the boat and parted ways. Johnny was on fire the whole ride home.

"Aw mate, that Maarja's a fuckin' looka," he kept saying.

I blew on my fingernails like "Yeah, I know." Inside, I was snakes and worms. I took a nap at Ralf's to get my head right. I showered my body, shaved my dome, and dressed my bites. The swelling had gone down; when I put on my visor, I looked normal. I asked Johnny to help with my wardrobe. I laid out my options on the bed. It was

---

[101] "In like Flynn" is a phrase which means to have quick success, usually in a romantic or sexual context. It is allegedly a reference to 1930s Australian actor, Errol Flynn, who was famous for his roles as a swashbuckler in films such as *The Adventures of Robin Hood* and *Captain Blood*. Flynn had a reputation as a hard-drinking, hellraising, ladies man with an enormous cock. He wrote an autobiography called *My Wicked, Wicked Ways* and was acquitted in February 1943 for the statutory rape of a teenage girl.

between the blue flannel and the gray. He pointed to the latter.

"Should prolly go with the one that isn't spotted with tomato sauce."[102]

I laughed and grabbed it. I slipped it on, along with my jeans. I clasped my Turkish gold chain around my neck. I donned my socks and Vans[103] and stood in the mirror. I didn't look half bad. Johnny agreed.

We pulled up to Loku at eight. It was a two-story bar with neon lights, a balcony, and a terrace. We entered and went upstairs. Johann and Maarja sat on white leather couches around a glass coffee table. Johann was in a black suit and tie. Maarja was wearing a blue denim jacket and tight jeans. I said hi to her and sat. We ordered drinks and chatted. I blabbed till I made her laugh. Then I looked at her slyly.

"So, what's this condition?"

She sipped her drink.

"You know Estonian language. But you don't know Estonian tradition. Here, if man wants to date woman, he must do three things. First, he must show he can drink. Second, he must show he can be gentleman. Third, he must show he can move. And this means dancing."

I knew I had the first one down cold. I was iffy on the second, but I knew I could learn. The third made me break into sweats. Sure, I could shimmy my shoulders and do a few steps, but I had zero skill, let alone moves. I stiffened my lips and nodded. I asked her what the next step was. She finished her drink.

"Since you are Mexican, we will order tequila. When I take sip, you take shot. And you will pay, of course."

"Of course."

---

[102] Australian-English term for ketchup.

[103] American manufacturer of sports shoes and apparel. It was started in Anaheim, California, in 1966.

She ordered twenty shots of Patrón Silver.[104] We each took one and toasted. She put the glass to her lips. She looked at me and sipped. I nodded and gulped my shot. It burned like ice. I grabbed a lime and bit it. Maarja sipped again. I necked another shot. This went on and on. By shot fifteen I was hammered. I could barely keep my eyes open. The whole table laughed. I asked Maarja if I'd done my duty. Her face warped and wobbled.

"I suppose."

She grabbed her purse and stood. She told me to call her tomorrow. I nodded and ran to the bathroom. I puked and puked. I returned and she was gone. The bill was on the table. It was 180 bucks. I paid it with a grunt. I got in the car with my buddies. Ralf was good to drive. We made off toward his house. Johnny was on me the whole way. He kept telling me I was in. I feigned excitement and tried not to yack. I made it to Ralf's house. I cupped my mouth and ran inside. I stumbled to the upstairs bathroom. I dropped to my knees and let it fly. The vomit ripped outta me like frightened cats from a paper bag. It slapped the water and churned. I heaved till my stomach was a bum's pocket. I looked at the light, saw double, and blacked out.

The next morning, I was a wreck. My veins were pumping dumpster juice and my head was a crushed pumpkin. I guzzled water, popped Tylenol, and chucked.[105] I rose in the afternoon, shaken but able. Johnny was on the phone with the ticket agency. He was trying to book a flight to Brazil via Germany in two days. He dicked around for an

---

[104] Premium brand of tequila products of 40% alcohol manufactured by the Patrón Spirits Company. It was introduced in 1989 and popularized in the early 2000s though repeated references by hip hop singers, the most notable of whom was Lil Jon.

[105] To chill with gusto; to unwind completely and let the stress of the day dribble from your joints; to sleep, especially peacefully. Highly relaxed; comfortable; tired; exhausted (*adj.*). A member of our group (*n.*).

hour. He got it done and hung up. He looked at me and grinned.

"You ready for tonight?"

I groaned and rolled over. He poked me outta bed and gave me his phone. I grabbed Maarja's number and called her. She told me to meet her at a restaurant in town called Stravinsky.[106] I said okay and hung up. I looked at my clothing situation. It was grim to none. I wished I had a gun. I asked Johnny if he could spare something. He rooted through his bag.

"Sorry to disappoint ya, but my stuff is dirty. I can loan ya my shoes and take ya clothes shopping tomorrow."

I thanked him for the gesture. I showered and shaved and cleaned the ketchup stains off my blue flannel. I put it on with some jeans and Johnny's black shoes. I looked like a hobo at a job interview. Johnny gave me a pep talk. It made me feel better. I went downstairs and grabbed my coat. Ralf called me a cab. I got to the restaurant on time. Maarja showed up a minute later. She wore red high heels and a flowered dress. I complimented her graciously. She thanked me and handed me her purse. I took it and opened the door. I followed her inside and looked at the place. It had mahogany carvings and crystal chandeliers. She'd reserved a table. I pulled out her chair and put her purse on the knob. She thanked me and sat. I sat next to her, and the waiter came. Maarja ordered a white wine and the salmon penne. I ordered a bottle of water and a bowl of chicken soup. She asked how I was feeling.

"Not so good," I said.

"That's okay. You only have to be gentlemen."

---

[106] Igor Fyodorovich Stravinsky (June 17, 1882 – April 6, 1971) was a Russian composer, pianist, and conductor. He is widely considered one of the most important and influential composers of the 20th century. His most famous ballet, *The Rite of Spring,* transformed the way in which subsequent composers thought about rhythmic structure and caused a near-riot at its premiere at the *Théâtre des Champs-Élysées* on May 29, 1913.

I raised a withered smile. I prayed I wouldn't have to lick the ground she walked on and let her use my back as a footrest. The woman took it easy on me. I had to ooh and ahh while she yammered on about being a model for Saku Beer,[107] plus I paid the exorbitant dinner bill, but after that, I was in the clear.

We grabbed our stuff and left the restaurant. I waited with her on the curb while she hailed a cab. I asked her when I'd see her again. A taxi pulled up and she opened the door.

"Call me tomorrow. You will take me to movie and sushi. Then I will see how you move."

I said okay, and she sped away. I got my own cab, cut to Ralf's, and crashed.

I woke up with a clean system. I bic'd my head and scrubbed my balls and gave Johnny the lowdown. I told him tonight was dance night. I asked him to show me some moves. He laughed and stood next to me. He zipped his feet into curlicues and told me to repeat. I made a few wobbly blobs. He pointed out my errors and showed me the way. I tried a few times and got it right. We moved on to leading and weaving and bumping and grinding.

By the end of the lesson, I felt confident. It was time to get clothes. We rousted Ralf and went to the mall. We picked out jeans, a collared shirt, and a clean pair of shoes. I dropped everything on my card. I went back to the crib and called Maarja. She told me to meet her at the theater at three. I said yippee and agreed. I slipped on my threads and my brand-new kicks. I practiced my dance moves and spritzed cologne on my tits. I looked in the mirror and adjusted my chain. I was a good-lookin' man,

---

[107] Estonian brewery and soft drinks company founded in 1820 and based in the small town of Saku. Since its inception, it has remained one of the leading breweries in the country.

minus the hairline. I popped on my visor for good measure. I had a celebratory shot of vodka with the boys before I left. The news was on the kitchen radio. The report was in Estonian and sounded urgent. I asked Ralf what the announcer was babbling about. He chuckled and waved the air.

"Oh, it is bullshit report that they find asteroid that will maybe hit earth in nineteen years."

The news struck me like a tomahawk to the groin. I broke into shakes and sweated. I tried to maintain my composure. It was like trying to build a house out of cornflakes in the rain. My friends asked me if I was okay. I told them I was fine and to call a cab. Ralf did so reluctantly. It came five minutes later.

On the way to the theater, I was a disaster. My heart was beating wildly, and my mind was racing. I imagined that asteroid hurtling toward earth. It didn't matter that it was nineteen years away, it could still hit the planet and explode it into molten stardust.

I arrived at the theater at three. I paid the cabbie and met my date at the door. I tried to look cool. My nerves were blown fuses and my spine was a blade of TV static. Maarja's outfit made it worse. She wore skintight jeans and a white V-neck that showed tons of cleavage. I simpered and ushered her in. She asked me what was wrong. I told her about the asteroid.

"That's silly," she said.

I insisted that it wasn't—that we could all die in a blaze of hellfire in nineteen little years. I asked her how she planned to live her life from now until then.

"I don't know. But right now, I want to see *Men in Black II*. Would you please pay the tickets?"

I paid the dude, and he unhooked the rope. We got snacks and walked to our theater. We sat in the front row. The lights dimmed and the reel spun. I mumbled and jittered and twitched. Maarja ate popcorn and ignored me.

I tried to concentrate on the film. Its subject matter heightened my anxiety. I went to the bathroom and washed my face. I looked in the mirror and saw my reflection. Disease had become a hideous infection. My face was a mess of craters, and my eyes were bleeding pustules. I washed it again and returned to my seat. Maarja implored me to calm down. I told her I was doing my best. The movie ended and we went to sushi. Before we got the menu, I ordered a double vodka. I inhaled it and ordered three more. The waiter brought our sushi boat. I was steaming drunk. Maarja smiled plastically and tried to make conversation. She bragged about how she'd had the highest IQ in her fifth-grade class. I asked her what it was. She squared her shoulders.

"One-thirty-five."

"Not bad."

Her eyes blipped.

"Not bad?" she said. "What is your IQ then?"

I downed another double and filled my maw with sushi.

"Wub-eighty."

Her mouth and eyes fell open. Her face looked like a network of bat caves. I chewed my food and smiled, all the while knowing that my score was the result of one shitty internet test I'd cheated on. I closed my mouth and swallowed. I drank more vodka and ate more sushi. Maarja kept staring.

"You're the smartest person I've ever met," she said.

I picked my teeth with my straw and burped.

"Thanks. And you're the prettiest."

She squeezed her tits together and blushed. I drank a few more vodkas. I paid the bill and walked her outside. She put on her coat and wriggled her shoulders.

"Are you ready to *move*?" she asked.

"Of course."

We walked down the cobblestone toward Krush. I tried

to remember my moves. I did a little two-step. I tripped on a stone and pitched forward. The corner of a flower trough caught my temple. It ripped open my scalp and took a chunk of skin with it. I slapped the wound and screamed. Blood gushed through the slots in my hand. Maarja gasped and gave me a tissue. I grabbed it and mopped the mess. We came to a square with a fountain. I sat on the lip and held my head. My arm was running with blood. My shirt and visor were destroyed, and my jeans were flecked red. Maarja folded her arms and looked at me. I was the sorriest soul in all of Tallinn. I prayed she'd take pity. Her eyes filled with something else. She leaned over and kissed my cheek.

"Good luck, Johann."

She turned and walked into the night. I sat on that fountain lip and cried myself to sleep.

CIAO, NIGGA

Rio de Janeiro—the name evokes images of sex, coke, and heat, Copacabana Beach with rows of plump, tanning asses, and loads of reckless debauchery. We wanted it all for our college summer trip, but it was 1:00 a.m. on our first night, and the closest Mason, Brendon, Steve, and I had come to experiencing Rio's bounty was sipping watery rum at a pisshole called Club Americano.

We sat at a table with a group of whores. They had haggard faces and wrinkled boobs and nails like glittery fishhooks. Steve ordered drinks for half of them.

"Shouldn't you be saving your fuckin' money?" I asked. "We're gonna be here two weeks, and you've already dropped a third of your budget."

He ran his fingers through his frizzy red hair.

"Fuck it. I'm getting married in a month. I'll eat street food the rest of the trip."

"Suit yourself."

We nursed our drinks. The strobe lights flashed, and the tinsel glinted. Fat assholes dripping with religious jewelry danced with skinny hookers in tube tops. The DJ stood in his booth and shouted a string of nonsensical profanities: "I fuck you. You fuck me. We fuck her. He fuck us." The ridiculousness made us laugh. We got up and hit the dancefloor. Steve and Mason grabbed a couple brunettes. Brendon and I took a pair of blondes. We all danced. My girl rubbed her knee against my crotch and winked.

"Buy me drink?" she asked.

"Why not."

We sat at our table. I called the waiter over and my date ordered. The waiter came back with iced tea in a shot glass.

"Fifteen dollars, plis," he said.

"Jesus Christ," I said, reaching into my pocket. I handed him the money sans tip. My girl touched my cheek and grinned with dishwater teeth.

"*Você é maravillhoso,*" she said. You're wonderful.

"*Obrigado.*"

At 3:00 a.m., I called it a night. Brendon joined me as he, too, was tired of the scene. We said late to Mason and Steve; they were knee-deep in whores. We made for the hotel. We walked under the fronds of a low-hanging palm. I kicked a beer can and burped.

"This fuckin' blows," I said. "I haven't gotten laid in *dayz*. I thought this trip was gonna fix that, but I guess not."

I dropped my head between my shoulders. Brendon chuckled.

"How long's it been?" he asked.

I raised four fingers.

"Damn, four months?"

I shook my head.

"Four years?"

I nodded.

"Holy fuck, dude."

I looked up expecting to see him smirk. His mouth was a wavy smudge, and his eyes were replete with sympathy. He ripped off his tank top and slung it over his shoulder.

"Let's get you some pussy."

We strutted back to the Copacabana strip. We ran into Steve, Mason, and their two blond trophies. They were on their way to our hotel. The girls batted their lashes and laughed at Steve's corny jokes. This got us juiced. We scanned the scene for options. We tried a few bars, but they were closed. The only place open was a restaurant with outdoor seating. We grabbed a table and ordered beers. From the corner of my eye, I saw two chicks giggling. I nudged Brendon.

"They're checkin' us out, man."

He looked over his shoulder. "Here they come," he mumbled. I felt a twitch in my crotch. It spread over my loins and through my taint, around my balls, and up my shaft. Like a cadaver zapped with electricity, my cock sprang to life. He shook the cobwebs from his shoulders and blinked the crust from his eye. He poked his head through the slit in my shorts.

Yo asshole, he called. *I've just spent a half-decade stuck to the side of your leg. Think we could get some pussy tonight?*

I pinched his neck and stuffed him back in my shorts. The ladies arrived at our table. One was tan with big titties and an ass you could bounce quarters off. She smiled and gave me her hand.

"Nice to meetchu," she said. "I am Branca."

She sat next to me. Brendon scowled at his leftovers. Her name was Morena. She bore a striking resemblance to Koko the talking gorilla. She wrapped her meaty arms around his neck and breathed in his ear. He cringed and swallowed his puke spittle. Branca and I munched chicken wings and exchanged glances. I felt precious about my change in luck.

At 4:00 a.m., we got in Branca's red Citroën. We drove off the strip and into a thicket of rundown block apartments. The ladies sat in front and chattered in Portuguese. I could barely make out a word. Brendon clenched his jaw and stared at his thumbs. I couldn't place his trepidation.

We arrived twenty minutes later. Their apartment building was tall, black, and ominous. We got out of the car and went inside. The night guard tipped his hat at Branca as we walked by. This puzzled me. We got in the elevator and went to the top floor. We walked down the hall to Branca's door. She keyed it and let us in. I saw a big-screen TV surrounded by seven smaller TVs; each had a camera view of an angle of the complex. I looked at Branca.

"What the hell is this?"

She flipped her juicy curls over her shoulder. "I am da boss of dis place," she said.

I looked around her flat. It had two master bedrooms, a huge bathroom, a full kitchen, a wide dining room, and was loaded with gaudy furniture, exotic plants, and paintings of African queens. She lit some candles and offered us a seat at her mahogany dinner table.

"We gotta good weed. Ya wanna smoke?"

"Fuck yeah," Brendon said.

She busted out a sack of green and twisted a blunt. She held it to her lips and sparked it. She looked like a smoking thug in a dark alley. She took a mean hit and passed it to Brendon. He puffed and puffed. Branca tilted her head back and opened her mouth. Smoke slithered up from her lips. Her eyes rolled white and flickered under her lids. My dick got shifty. He tapped me on the belly and poked his head out my shorts.

I'm warning you, Johann. If I'm not diving headfirst into a soaking vagina by five a.m., me and the balls are packin' up and movin' south.

I swallowed the lump in my throat and looked at Brendon. He was staring at his forearms and frowning. Morena was caressing his face and brandishing her yellowed fronts. He slapped her hand away.

"I gotta yack."

He lifted himself and stumbled to the bathroom. We heard a loud burp followed by the sound of chunks hitting water. The toilet flushed. Brendon came out with tears in his eyes.

"Sorry about that," he said.

Morena batted her camel lashes. She stood and dragged him by the arm toward her room. Branca took my hand and led me toward her room on the opposite end of the hall. I looked at Brendon one last time.

"I'm nervous, dude," I said.

His face went from green to red.

"You better get in there and tear that pussy up."

"Why?"

"Because," he said, as the door eclipsed his face. "I'm about to swallow a turd for you."

My heart fluttered and my palms pooled with sweat. Branca closed the door behind me. She peeled her clothes off slowly. She wore black lace lingerie underneath. Her breasts hung in her bra like ripe mangoes. Her ass sat in her thong with perfect symmetry. She struck a pose and ran her hands down her body. I crossed myself and dropped my drawers. I mounted her and thrust my cock in her vagina. The force of our clapping bodies slammed the headboard against the wall. I felt an orgasm approaching. My limbs rattled like tin cans in the wind. I arched my back and clenched my butt cheeks. She reached around and stuffed her index finger in my asshole. I grunted and slapped her hand away. My organism receded. I pumped harder and harder. She told me to calm down. I didn't listen. She jammed her finger up my ass again. My cock deflated into a wrinkled nub. I dismounted and rolled over.

"When was da las' time you made love?" she asked.

"Eight months."

She raised an eyebrow. I lifted the head of my penis and jiggled it.

"Would you mind sucking him back to life?"

She huffed. "I never suck on da firs' date."

"This is a date?"

"You know my meaning."

We settled on a handjob. She lathered me up and yanked me around. I couldn't nut. We called it quits after a few minutes. We cuddled awkwardly. We closed our eyes and went to sleep.

I crawled out of bed at ten and went into the hall. Morena emerged from her room wearing only Brendon's NorCal T-shirt. Her hair shot in every direction. Her ass cheeks wobbled and jiggled. I went into her room and found Brendon zipping up his pants.

"How was it?" I asked.

"It was ait actually. She gave me a sloppy BJ and I hit it standing up. Girl fucks like a savage. How was Branca?"

"She fingered my asshole."

"It's tight, huh? Hella makes you bust hardcore."

"I guess."

We went to the living room and sat on the couch. Branca was in the kitchen making coffee. She came in and greeted us. Then she hit us up for twenty bucks.

"What for?" I asked.

She gave me a dirty look. Before she could respond, her cellphone rang. She looked at the face and answered it.

"Estou. O que você quer?"

She yelled with all her lungpower. The vein on her neck bulged. The person on the other end yelled back. It sounded like a drug deal gone sour. She pressed her mouth into a ball. A moment of silence ensued. She took the phone from her ear and held it to her lips.

"Ciao, nigga," she shouted.

That was our cue. We paid her the money and cut.

CAFÉ CON LECHE

Joe met Mina in Granada.[108] She was his friend Ramon's girl, but Joe didn't care; he fell for her the second he saw her. She was tall and slender with green eyes and brown hair. Her smile danced across her face when she laughed. She had copper skin and a perfect ass. One night while Ramon was away in Córdoba,[109] Joe and Mina met for a walk. The moon shone in the sky like a polished opal, lining the pinpricks in the night with blue. They walked down a cobbled lane and chatted. Joe was a wreck from his recent breakup.

"She stomped my heart bloody," he said.

Mina slid her fingers down his cheek. "Don' worry abou' that. It will pass."

Her words were like cool water in a dry mouth. His chest swelled. He took a deep breath and steadied himself. He leaned into her ear.

"I love you," he said.

She reached out and hugged him. He could feel her shaking.

---

[108] Capital city of the province of Granada, in the autonomous community of Andalusia, Spain. It is home to the Alhambra, the most renowned building of the Moorish occupation of Spain. It is also the birthplace of world-famous *matador* (bullfighter) David Fandila Marín, known as "El Fandi."

[109] City in Andalusia, southern Spain, and the capital of the province of Córdoba. It has many notable examples of Moorish architecture, such as the Mezquita, which was a mosque during the Moorish occupation, but was later converted into a cathedral.

"Iss so fucking unfair," she cried. "Please understan' tho. I am in loff with Ramon."

Ramon was a player down to his socks. He was probably fucking another broad in Córdoba as they spoke. Joe unhooked Mina's arms and stood back.

"I guess we'll just be friends."

They kept in touch for a while. Joe was an avid traveler and sent Mina handwritten letters from abroad. She responded with flirtatious emails. He tried to ignore them. Eventually, he stopped writing her. She was a seed of pain he locked in his heart. He almost forgot about her. One day, his phone rang.

"Hello?"

"Yoe? Iss Mina. Dju remember me?"

The seed blossomed into needles.

"Hi, Mina."

"I'm coming to California nex' week. I wanna see dju."

Ramon had recently moved to LA; Joe knew she'd visit him first. He thought of Ramon's cock filling her mouth with cum. He squeezed his face into a dot.

"Are dju there?"

"Yes."

"Can I come stay with dju?"

"I guess."

"Fantastico. Oh, Yoe, I can' wait."

"Me neither."

He went to the liquor store and bought a case of cheap wine. He took it to his flat and drank. He thought of his ex and what a manipulative cunt she'd been. He thought of his dead-end job and estranged family. He thought of Mina and her dick-teasing. It disgusted him to think he'd give in to it while her pussy was still wet for Ramon. He felt small enough to slip through the floorboards.

"I need one thing of my own," he croaked.

He woke up a week later in a pool of vomit. A shoebox was resting near his head. Polaroids of him and Mina were scattered around it. He pried himself from the floor, put the Polaroids in the box, and placed it gently on a shelf. He went to the bathroom and washed his face. His phone buzzed.

"I am at airport in San Francisco," Mina wrote. "Come to get me?"

He groaned and got in his Pinto. He drove through his crummy neighborhood and across the bay to SFO.[110] Mina was at the curb with her bags. She wore a white dress with spaghetti straps. Her brown hair ran down her shoulders. Her smile danced like a flag. She threw her arms around him.

"Yoe," she cried.

He hugged her weakly and pulled away. She looked into his eyes.

"Dju miss me?"

"Something like that."

He loaded her bags and they took off. Mina chattered about her life. Joe listened with one ear. He knew it was gonna be a long night. Mina finished talking about herself. She switched to hounding him about the places he'd been. She had a similar passion for travel. But teaching Salsa didn't afford her the same mobility that freelance journalism afforded him. He described a few spots. He left out the juicy details. They arrived at his shabby apartment building. He carried Mina's bags up the steps. He keyed his door and offered her his room. She accepted without protest.

"So wha' now?" she asked.

"Wanna party?"

"*Por supuesto.*"

They went on his little balcony. He cracked a bottle of wine and packed his hookah. The night air was cool. The stars were gem flecks, and the moon was a slice of electric

---

[110] San Francisco International Airport.

cheese. Joe blew smoke rings over the railing. Mina recounted a boat trip she had taken off the coast of Spain.

"I met one boy and we khad beautiful loff together. But then it wass over and khee wass very angry to me."

She looked at Joe. He gulped his wine.

"Well," she said. "I tol' dju one off my trawel stories. Will dju tell me one off djors?"

"My travels are boring compared to yours. You keep going."

She shrugged and sipped her wine.

"Okay."

She proceeded to list all the men she'd slept with since she and Ramon had had their "temporary separation." It was an endless string of Eduardos, Enriques, Filipes, and Juans. Every time she named a new guy, Joe took a swig. He drank himself cross-eyed.

"Okay, enough abou' me. Dju tell me something abou' djor traweling."

Joe quaffed his glass and shakily poured another. An idea came.

"Wanna hear the story of a girl named Valeria?" he said, trying not to slur.

"*¡Si!*"

"Okay. I met her in Peru in '03. She was getting married to another guy, but I didn't care. She had the cutest little crooked mouth. And when I teased her, she gave me an elbow and said *Ozhe.* We spent four days together wandering the streets of Lima. We got to know each other super well. I eventually convinced her to kiss me. We made love a day later. I was so depressed saying goodbye. She stood on the curb with her hands folded, staring at me with her big brown eyes. I whimpered and got in a cab. I remember the driver's first words to me were 'Ah, *el amor.*' His name was Macho, and to console me, he told me the story of a woman he loved. 'I called her my *café con leche,*' he said. 'Because she used to make milk coffee for me every morning when I was hungover.' He said they were lovers through their teens and twenties, that they broke up and he ran through a lot of shitty women afterward. Then one day she came back into his life. They got married and had kids and were happy ever after. Macho told me not to worry. And whatever I did, I had to call him when I found my café con leche."

Mina smiled. "That wass a wonderful story."

Joe looked in her eyes; they were swirls of green mirror flakes. They sucked him from his seat. He puckered his lips and put them to hers. She closed her mouth and ducked. His lips smeared across her forehead. He fell back in his seat.

"Ai'n so sorry," she said.

He took his glass and stared at it. He focused on the splotch of wine jiggling at the bottom. Mina put her hand on his shoulder.

"Don' worry. Dju will find djor café con leche."

A smile was slithering across her face. Joe put down his glass and stood.

"I'll be right back."

He walked inside and fumbled around. He came out with his shoebox. He sat and placed it on his lap.

"I will have my one thing."

"Wha'?" Mina said.

He ignored her and stared at the box. He took a deep breath and opened it. Mina smiled. Then she gasped.

"Yoe, what are dju doing?" she cried.

He reached in and grabbed the pistol amidst the Polaroids. He lifted it to his temple and shot his brains across her pretty white dress.

THE BROWNIE INCIDENT

I slouched on my parents' sofa and watched empty-calorie–TV. I was still jetlagged, having returned from Spain a week earlier. I dozed during the climactic interlude between *ElimiDate*[111] and *Blind Date.*[112] I heard a knock at the front door. I groaned and stood. I went to the door and opened it. It was my buddy, Mason. He waltzed in with a JanSport[113] on his back.

"I got a little surprise for you," he said.

He unzipped his backpack and pulled out a wad of tinfoil; I snatched it from his hand and opened it. A cube of green-tinted chocolate was inside.

"I just picked it up from the clinic," he said. "It's poty[114] as hell though. Won't take much to fuck you up. *Especially you.*"

---

[111] American reality television dating show in which one contestant chose between four contestants of the opposite sex by eliminating them one by one in three total rounds. It premiered on September 17, 2001, and it went out of syndication after September 5, 2006.

[112] American dating game show in which people who did not previously know each other are paired and sent on a blind date. The cameras follow them around while commentary in the form of subtitles, animations, and "thought bubbles" are later added by the show's producers. The show was originally hosted by Roger Lodge (1999-2006) and is currently hosted by comedian Nikki Glaser (2019 – present).

[113] American brand of backpacks and collegiate apparel, which is now owned by VF Corporation. It is the world's largest backpack maker, and together with The North Face (also owned by VF Corporation) sells nearly half of all small backpacks sold in the United States. The company was founded in 1967 in Seattle, Washington. Its biggest innovation was the panel-loading daypack, which opposed the ubiquitous top-loading packs of the time.

[114] Potent; strong.

I had never tried pot brownies. The last time I smoked was in eighth grade. Weed didn't sit well with me. I either lay around muttering or spent the night screaming at the toilet bowl. I was determined to change that. I broke off a chunk, popped it in my mouth, and chewed. I could taste the crystals of THC[115] mixed with the chocolate.

"When will I feel it?"

"Give it an hour. But don't wait for it to happen. Let it creep naturally."

"Ait."

He inhaled half the brownie. We put on *Scarface*[116] and kicked back. Everything was gravy. We ate Cheetos and enjoyed the flick. An hour rolled by. I still hadn't felt a head change. I looked over at Mason.

"Lemme get another nug'a that shit."

He glanced at me. His expression was a mix of uncertainty and morbid curiosity.

"Go ahead."

I grabbed a hunk and scarfed it. I nestled in and watched the film. A tingling sensation crawled up my spine. I twisted my neck and squinted my eyes. Al Pacino cruised around on the screen in a white Caddie. He yelled,

---

[115] Principal psychoactive constituent of cannabis—one of at least 113 total cannabinoids identified in the plant—and the responsible element for untold millions of trips. Although the chemical formula for THC ($C_{21}H_{30}O_2$) describes multiple isomers, the term THC usually refers to the Delta-9-THC isomer with chemical name (−)-trans-Δ9-tetrahydrocannabinol. Like most pharmacologically active secondary metabolites of plants, THC is a lipid found in cannabis, assumed to be involved in the plant's evolutionary adaptation, putatively against insect predation, ultraviolet light, environmental stress, and human consumption (whoops).

[116] American crime drama film directed by Brian De Palma and written by Oliver Stone. A remake of the 1932 film of the same name, it tells the story of Cuban refugee Tony Montana (Al Pacino), who arrives penniless in 1980s Miami and goes on to become a powerful and ruthless drug lord. Initial critical reception was negative due to its excessive violence, profanity, and drug use. In the years that followed, critics reappraised it, and it is now considered one of the greatest gangster films ever made.

"You cock-a-roaches." A surge of giggles burst from my mouth. I pounded the cushion and shouted, "Al Pacino's blowin' it up, hahahaha."

I could barely finish my sentence. Mason grunted disinterestedly. I leaned back to shout again. My consciousness flickered like an antique lightbulb. Reality arrived in chewed puzzle pieces. My heart clawed at the bottom of my throat. I turned to Mason in panic.

"I think I ate too much," I whispered.

"You're fine, dude," he said, yawning. "Just chuck."

I stood and paced the room. I held a hand to my chest. My heart clapped like a thundercloud.

"I think I'm having a heart attack!"

Mason looked at me with bloodshot eyes. "I think Al Pacino's in Bolivia."

I stamped my feet and grabbed the phone. I quickly dialed 911. Mason paused the movie.

"What the hell are you doing?" he said.

I held the phone to my ear. It rang and rang. A woman answered.

"Nine-one-one, what is your emergency?"

"I'm having a heart attack," I screamed. "I live at two-twenty-two Schenectady Lane. Send somebody right away."

The last word left my mouth and reason kicked in. The anxiety drained from my body and my head cleared. I realized what I'd done.

"Never mind," I told the operator. "I'm just a little panicky. Please don't send an ambulance."

"We've already dispatched one, sir. I can't recall it."

I groaned and hung up. Two minutes later, the air throbbed with sirens. I stumbled outside. An ambulance with spinning red lights screeched to a halt in front of my house. Six EMTs hopped out. I stood dumbfounded. An EMT approached me, carrying a first aid kit. He was a lanky black man with a bald head and a stern face. He looked like an African general.

"You the one who called about the heart attack?" he said.

"Um, yes?"

He grabbed me by the elbow and took me into the house. He sat me on the couch and whistled in his friends. They flooded my living room with a crackling of walkie-talkies. They brought syringes, breathing masks, stethoscopes, a stretcher, and a heart monitor. They ripped open my shirt and attached leach-like electrodes. I heard my dog bark in the kitchen. Mason shushed her. I prayed my parents were still asleep upstairs.

"Your heart's beatin' like a hummingbird," the general said. "But you ain't havin' no heart attack."

"Is anybody here with you?" another EMT asked.

"Uh, my dog Buffster."

The EMT raised his eyebrows. "This kid's off his rocker," he whispered.

"Son, do you take any medication?" the general asked me.

My head wobbled in its socket. "Do gummy vitamins count?"

He snickered and reached in his pocket. He pulled out his flashlight and clicked it at my pupils. He raised a half-smile.

"We're done here, gentlemen," he said.

People chuckled and cleared out. I signed a waiver and handed it to the general. He took it and bounced. I stood and schlepped back to the family room. Mason looked at me from the sofa.

"Are you a genius?" he asked.

"Whatever, man."

I plopped in my seat and leaned back. The shock subsided and the weed took over. My mind detached from its root. My eyes melted down my cheeks. My body turned heavy as granite. I looked at Mason and smiled.

"I never knew it could be so wonderful," I crooned.

He chuckled and nodded. I turned my head and closed my eyes. I saw vibrant mosaics of color. I felt simple and serene. Tiny high-pitched voices screamed, "Sunshine. Sunshine. Sunshine." Through golden reeds, a figure appeared. He was a tall black man in a white suit. He had long legs, a neat beard, and an afro that blew up from his head like a tumbleweed. He lay in a canoe and strummed a guitar. A rainbow waterfall whooshed behind him.

"Hey, man," he said. "I been waitin' on you."

He had the voice of an ancient redwood. I walked closer.

"You a high-strung cat."

"I know," I replied. "I always have been. Especially when things are out of my control."

"Wha'chu need to do is chill out and let yo' mind take you for a ride. Otherwise, you gon' go crazy."

"Okay," I said, nodding. "But I have a question."

"Whassat?"

"Who the fuck are you?"

He smiled like a distant memory—one stuffed way back in the brain closet like the rhinestone jacket of a dead relative. I stared at him in a daze. His gaze played Tetris with my DNA. The scene slowly faded. I opened my eyes and saw Mason snoring into a pillow. I stood and clicked off the TV. I staggered upstairs and crashed.

I woke up groggy. I drank a tall glass of tap water and washed my face. I hobbled downstairs to the kitchen. My mother was at the stove and my father was at the table. They looked up from what they were doing and stared at me. I readied myself for the knife. My mom smiled.

"Would you like some eggs, sweetie?"

HOOKED

PART ONE

I walked up the steps to my classroom and through the open door. I wore a beanie over my eyebrows and a checkered flannel. My jeans sagged and my shoes were unlaced. My earphones were clamped around my head like electro-shock nodes. I took a front seat and pulled out my binder. The teacher stood from her chair. She was stalky and brown. Ringlets of black hair were pasted to her scalp. She fixed her glasses and grabbed the chalk.

"My name is Señora Lopez," she said, writing. "But y'all can call me Gabi."

She cut into Spanish. It was faster than the high school shit I was used to. I jotted everything I could. I had to make grade or my university would put the kibosh on my plans to study in Madrid that fall. Gabi listed off authors we'd be reading: Juan Rulfo,[117] Pablo Neruda,[118]

---

[117] Mexican author, screenwriter, and photographer (May 16, 1917 – January 7, 1986). Best known for *Pedro Páramo* (1955), a short novel about a man named Juan Preciado who travels to Comala—his recently deceased mother's hometown—to meet his father. Upon arrival, he finds that the town is populated only by ghosts of the deceased, who take turns narrating the story from their perspective.

[118] Chilean poet, diplomat, and politician (July 12, 1904 – September 23, 1973) who won the Nobel Prize for Literature in 1971. Pablo Neruda's father opposed his son's interest in writing; however, he received encouragement from others, including the future Nobel Prize winner Gabriela Mistral. In 1924, Neruda published *Veinte poemas de*

Federico Lorca,[119] Gabriel García Márquez.[120] From the corner of my eye, I saw a hand go up. Gabi pointed to it and nodded.

"Are we gonna read anything that isn't written by crusty old men?" the girl asked.

A few students laughed. I turned around and checked the source. She was tall, skinny, and tan. She wore blue jeans on her long legs and a black top that exposed her belly button and made her nipples pop. Her ears and neck were decorated in moonstone jewelry. Her hair was butterscotch brown and ran down to her ass. She had close-set black eyes and a pointy nose. Her lips were thin and glossy and hung in a loose circle around her most prominent features. I'd call them teeth, but they transcended that title; the bottom row was like a graveyard

---

amor y una canción desesperada (Twenty Love Poems and A Desperate Song), a collection of love poems that was controversial for its eroticism, especially considering its author's young age. Over the decades, *Veinte poemas* sold millions of copies and became Neruda's best-known work. Today, it retains its place as the best-selling poetry book in the Spanish language.

[119] Andalusian poet, playwright, and theatre director. In 1919–20, he wrote and staged his first play, *The Butterfly's Evil Spell*, which dramatized the impossible love between a cockroach and a butterfly. An unappreciative public laughed it off the stage after only four performances. In 1928, García Lorca published *Romancero Gitano* (Gypsy Ballads), a highly stylized imitation of the ballads and poems from the Spanish countryside. The book brought him fame across Spain and the Hispanic world; it is considered his best work. At the beginning of the Spanish Civil War (1936), García Lorca was killed by Nationalist forces. His remains have never been found.

[120] Colombian novelist, short-story writer, screenwriter, and journalist. He is considered one of the most significant authors of the 20th century, particularly in the Spanish language, and was the 1982 recipient of the Nobel Prize in Literature. His grandmother, Doña, played an influential role in his writing. He was inspired by the way she "treated the extraordinary as something perfectly natural." Her house was filled with stories of ghosts, premonitions, omens, and portents. According to García Márquez, she was his "source of the magical, superstitious, and supernatural view of reality." He enjoyed his grandmother's unique way of telling stories; so much so that thirty years later, it heavily influenced his most popular novel, *One Hundred Years of Solitude* – a masterwork of magical realist style.

of bone dominoes, and the top row was like the polished railing of a marble balcony. I was immediately attracted to her. I stared at the V in her crotch. She waited for an answer. Gabi chuckled.

"Por supuesto," she said. "Isabel Allende[121] will feature heavily in our readings. As will Guadalupe Amor,[122] Rigoberta Menchú,[123] and Emilia Pardo Bazán."[124]

---

[121] Chilean writer (born August 2, 1942) who has been called "the world's most widely read Spanish-language author." Her novels are often based upon her personal experience and historical events, and pay homage to the lives of women, while weaving together elements of myth and realism. In 1973, she fled to Venezuela to avoid persecution under the Pinochet dictatorship. In 1981, while in Caracas, she received a phone call informing her that her 99-year-old grandfather was near death. She sat down to write him a letter, hoping to thereby "keep him alive, at least in spirit." The letter evolved into a book, *The House of the Spirits* (1982), which was intended to exorcise the ghosts of the Pinochet dictatorship. The book was rejected by numerous Latin American publishers but was eventually published in Buenos Aires. It was translated into a score of languages, becoming her most popular book.

[122] Mexican poet (born January 9, 1959) who wrote as Pita Amor. She was of mixed French, German, and Spanish ancestry and was known for her rebelliousness and audacious lifestyle. She was an actress and a model for famous photographers and painters such as Diego Rivera and Raúl Anguiano; she shocked her family and the Mexican public when it was revealed that she had posed in the nude. Her poetry is notable for its direct expressions about metaphysical issues such as human weakness. Some of her most famous books are *Puerta obstinada, Otro libro de amor, Todos los siglos del mundo,* and *Yo soy mi casa.*

[123] Guatemalan human rights activist, feminist, author (born January 9, 1959) and Nobel Peace Prize laureate (1992). She was born to a poor Indigenous family of K'iche' Maya descent in Laj Chimel, a rural area in north-central Guatemala. Most of her immediate family was killed during the Guatemalan Civil War (1960-1996). In 1982, she narrated a book about her life, titled *Me llamo Rigoberta Menchú y así me nació la conciencia* (My Name is Rigoberta Menchú, and this is how my Awareness was Born). Although she had only learned to speak it three years prior, Menchú narrated the book in Spanish—an effort to master the language of her oppressors and turn it against them. The book made her an international icon and brought attention to the suffering of Indigenous peoples under an oppressive government regime.

[124] Spanish novelist, journalist, literary critic, poet, playwright, translator, editor, and professor (September 16, 1851 – May 12, 1921).

"Praise Allah," the girl said.

Break came an hour later. Everybody went outside. I walked down the steps and away from the crowd. I posted against a concrete pillar and crossed one leg over the other. I adjusted my headphones and hit "play" on my Kenwood.[125] The song "Oh Boy"[126] filled my ears. I bobbed my head and mouthed the words. The girl broke from the herd and swished down the steps. I eyed her teeth and the V in her jeans. My sack tightened and my pecker stiffened. I rearranged myself and swallowed the lump in my throat. She walked to me and grabbed my CD player. She popped it open and saw the disc.

"Rap. Yuck," she said.

I flared one nostril and dipped the corresponding eyebrow. Her face morphed into a little girl's. She bulleted her tongue between her teeth and bobbled her head. She turned and bounced away.

"Fuckin' weirdo," I muttered.

I went back inside. We didn't look at each other for the

Known for introducing naturalism and feminist ideas into Spanish literature. Her father, believing in the intellectual equality of men and women, provided her education and inspired her love for literature. Her third novel, *La tribuna* (1883), described the development of a disheveled street urchin called Amparo, into a leader among the women in the factory where she worked. The book provoked much outrage among critics. Her husband was unwilling to weather the ensuing social scandal and two years later the couple separated. According to some, her naturalism was partially inspired by late 19th-century theories of racial heritage and atavism. Pardo Bazán was well-versed in the racial theories applied to criminology by Cesare Lombroso, and she regularly espoused racist views. She also held antisemitic ideas and tried to justify antisemitism in 1899 in the context of the Dreyfus affair.

[125] Japanese company that designed, developed, and marketed car, home, and personal audio, and professional and amateur radio communications equipment. The name Kenwood is a combination of "Ken," a name common to Japan and North America, and "Wood," suggesting a relation to Hollywood, California.

[126] "Oh Boy" is a 2002 Grammy-nominated hip hop single by Harlem-born rapper Cam'ron from his album *Come Home with Me*. It peaked at number four on the Billboard Hot 100 and ranked 89th on VH1's 100 Greatest Songs of Hip Hop.

rest of class. She approached me the next day at break. This time she was smiling.

"Don't you wanna know my name?" she asked.

"What?"

"My name. Don't you wanna know it?

"Umm."

"It's Tanya Gladstone, if you must know."

"Cool. I'm Johann."

"Johann what?"

"Felmanstien."

"Are you Jewish?"

"Nope. German-Mexican."

"Oh my God, we're twins!"

"Huh?"

"My mommy's Salvadorian, and my daddy's a Russian Jew."

"Great."

"Anyways, gimme that."

She plucked the Nokia from my flannel pocket. She held it to her face and picked at its belly with her spindly thumbs. She pressed Enter and handed it back to me.

"There. Now you have my number. We can be study buddies."

"Study buddies?"

"Yes. Now, if you don't mind, I hafta get back to class. Byeee."

She turned and bounced up the steps. I shook my head and followed.

We worked on a few projects, mostly in class or over the phone. One night, she invited me to her dorm. She told me to bring my notes and the book we were reading.

"But you can only stay for one hour. My boyfriend Danny will be here, and I haven't had his penis inside me for two weeks."

I almost dropped the phone.

"Why don't I come another night?"

"No. Our final book report is due this week. I wanna get that off my brain first. Plus, I want you to meet Danny."

"Whatever."

I grabbed my shit and drove to campus. I parked in front of UCSD's International House.[127] I got out and walked to the Norway Dorms. I knocked on number 2805. Tanya answered the door. She was wearing blue bellbottoms with gill-rips and a white blouse. Her nails were painted purple and her hair was in pigtails. An amethyst crystal dangled above her tits. She let me in and closed the door.

"Yeee," she said, giving me a hug.

I smelled weed. The door to her bedroom creaked open. A guy stood at the threshold in a haze of smoke. He was short and pasty with blond locks and green eyes. His chin and neck were covered in stubble. He wore a wrinkly gray T-shirt and holey jeans. Tanya turned around and pointed at him with her index fingers.

"Johann, this is Danny," she said. "And Danny, this is Johann."

She turned and pointed at me. I cocked a half-smile.

"Yo."

Danny flinched. Tanya rolled her eyes.

"Alright, silly. Get in bed and wait for me."

He did as he was told. Tanya and I sat down and worked. An hour later, she stood.

"Okay," she said, gripping the back of her neck. "It's time for yo' ass to go."

Her aura was tweaked—like someone had stabbed a rainbow in the red. The hair on my forearms rose. I stood and grabbed my bag. Tanya hugged me and went into her room.

---

[127] Part of Eleanor Roosevelt College at the University of California, San Diego. It consists of four apartment buildings whose residents are half international and half domestic students.

"You can see yourself out."

I tipped her two. She thinned her eyes and closed the door. I caught a glimpse of Danny. His face was whiter than creek rock.

The semester ended two weeks later. I went on a mad trip with some homies across South America, then I blasted off to Madrid. I drank and partied like a motherfucker. I did a little work too. I came back to Cali in December of '03. I was supposed to graduate in six months. I didn't have near enough credits; too much blowing up[128] and not enough studying. I hit a slump that had me poppin' pills and seein' a shrink. I thought I was going schizo, but my shrink said, "No, you just need to get busy." I took her words to heart. I mapped out my classes for year five and wrote for *The Guardian*.[129] I made staff writer in a month. By May, I was elected Features Editor for the coming school year. I was stoked to smoke the stars. All that in time for Sun God.[130] I went with some coworkers from the paper. We got shitfaced at a campus bar then hit RIMAC

---

[128] Party hard; to travel (the world); to fuck; to have intimate contact with; to do something wild or out of the ordinary to the umpteenth degree; to do or experience anything good or bad in an extreme or exaggerated sense.

[129] Student-operated newspaper at the University of California, San Diego. Originally named the *Triton Times* (after the university's mascot), it is published weekly during the regular academic year, usually on Mondays. Unlike many college newspapers, *The Guardian* has no faculty advisor and is not formally tied to any academic program.

[130] Annual campus festival at UCSD that takes place every spring quarter. It has featured a cross-campus fair, lounge areas, and performances, including live comedy, student talent, DJ sets, and concerts. The festival's name references the Sun God, a 14-foot (4.3 m) on-campus statue of a multicolored bird-like creature perched atop a 15-foot (4.6 m) tall arch-shaped, vine-covered concrete pedestal. The first Sun God Festival (1983) coincided with the one-year anniversary of the statue's arrival. Its original location was adjacent to the statue, but it has since grown and moved to RIMAC field.

Field.[131] Busta Rhymes[132] was headlining. We were just in time. We squeezed into the sea of people and red cups. The stage lit up and homeboy came out wearing a bib of diamonds and dreadlocks to his knees. He grabbed the mic and spit. The crowd went nuts. I shot my fist in the air. Someone tapped my shoulder. I turned around.

"Yeee," Tanya squeaked.

She was wearing a green top and jeans so tight they looked like body paint. Her butterscotch hair was draped over her left breast, making her right breast stand out. She bounced on the balls of her feet and smiled. When I didn't smile back, she covered her teeth with her lips. She looked like she had a plum in her mouth. I chuckled.

"It's good to see you, Tanya."

She smiled again and hugged me.

"Yay. Now squat, so I can get on yo' shoulders, mofo."

"I thought you hated rap?"

"I do. But I love to see all the peoples!"

"As you wish."

I got down and she climbed onto my shoulders. I grabbed her calves and stood. Her lower half was much heavier than her skinny torso betrayed. It was like lifting a scarecrow in lead pants. I felt the warmth of her crotch on my nape. I imagined how her pussy might taste. The

---

[131] Sports complex at UCSD comprising an arena, a weight room, and various other event and athletic facilities. It is one of the largest college athletic facilities in the US.

[132] American rapper (born May 20, 1972) who has received twelve Grammy nominations for his work, making him one of the most-nominated artists without winning. He is of Afro-Jamaican descent and identifies as a member of the Five-Percent Nation—an Islam-influenced, Black nationalist movement which was founded in 1964 in Harlem by Allah the Father (born Clarence Edward Smith). Members of the group believe that ten percent of the world's people know the truth of existence and opt to keep eighty-five percent of the world in ignorance and under their control; the remaining five percent (i.e. "The Five Percenters") also know the truth, but are determined to enlighten the eighty-five percent. Busta does this with his rap.

music for "Break Ya Neck"[133] played. It was my favorite Busta song. I rapped along with him. Tanya squealed and rubbed my scalp. Her fingers were like talons. They turned my spine to jelly. The song ended and I took a deep breath.

"That was awesome," she said. "I don't like rap, but when you rap, it puts me in a trance."

"Thanks."

The concert ended. Tanya climbed off and we left the arena. She pulled out a joint. She took a few puffs and offered it to me. I told her, "No thanks." She shrugged and took another puff. Her eyes were red as stop signs. She put her arms out and spun.

"I'm soooo stooooned."

She laughed and stumbled into me. I caught her with both arms. Her skin was hot to the touch. She looked up at me with her stop-sign eyes.

"I broke up with Danny," she said.

"Oh yeah?"

"Yeah. Poor thing. He was crushed. Anyways, we should go on a date. How's next Wednesday?"

"I'm free."

"Yay. I'll meet you at the food court for lunch."

We met that Wednesday at noon. We went to a Japanese joint with conveyor-belt sushi. We picked a few items and sat down. Tanya was wearing blue jeans, pink sneakers, and a black top with sleeves to her elbows. She chomped into a piece of *sake*.[134] Her lower jaw rotated as she chewed. Her upper jaw remained still. I stared at her wall

---

[133] Second single from Busta's fifth album *Genesis* (2001)—arguably his best. The song was produced by Dr. Dre and Scott Storch. It starts with an interpolation of the Red Hot Chili Peppers song "Give It Away," then busts into a flow that is one of hip hop's fastest and most complex. MCs who attempt to rap it could quiet possibly break their necks in the process.

[134] Japanese nigiri sushi consisting of hand-pressed sushi rice topped with slices of raw salmon.

of teeth. She thinned her eyes to slits. She scraped the back of her hand over her nostrils.

"You wanna sex me, don't you?" she asked, sniffling.

"Excuse me?"

"Don't be embarrassed. I wanna sex you too. But before we sex, there's three things you must know."

"I'm listening."

"The first thing is, I like girls."

"Okay?"

"I mean, I prefer penis, but I like da poosy too."

"I see."

"The second thing is—and this relates to the first—I'm very sexually open."

"What does that mean?

"It means I like to try new things in the bedroom."

"Alright. And the third?"

She leaned in and crossed her arms. She hooked her fingers under her sleeves and pulled them up to her shoulders. Her upper arms were covered in scars. They looked like little slugs stacked on top of one another. I feigned confusion. She rolled her eyes.

"I'm a cutter."

"Class or cheese?"

"Very funny. I'm sure you're not perfect either."

"I've been told otherwise."

"Ha. Finish yo' food. I'm horny."

We went to my place. My flatmates were still in class. We went up to my room and closed the door. We took off our shoes and lay on my bed. We embraced and made out. I undid her jeans and ran my hand down her panties. Her pussy was hot and gushy. It felt like a microwaved tulip. I fingered her clit. She detached her lips from mine and pulled her pants down.

"I want you to eat her," she said.

I was fully erect. I kneeled between her legs and slid off her panties. Her pussy was a clean-shaven oval. It sparkled with beads of juice. I leaned forward and sunk my face in. It smelled and tasted of rain. I went at it like a jackal with a carcass. She arched her back and moaned. I thought she was close. I stopped and looked at her.

"Keep going, foo!" she said.

I laughed and continued. She grabbed my fingers and guided them into her vagina. I felt a huge artery. It was like a swollen tree root. I rubbed it and sucked her clit. Her thighs vibrated around my head.

"I'm fucking coming," she yelled.

Her pussy gagged and convulsed. The bed shook. She squealed with pleasure. Then she went still.

"Well, that was decent. Now lemme do you."

I'd never been so thrilled about an insult. I pulled off my pants and boxers and lay back. Tanya straddled my hairy legs and stuck her ass in the air. I was a little worried about her teeth. She tucked them expertly and sucked. I put my hands behind my head and tried to relax. It felt like I was having dick surgery with local anesthesia. She stopped and looked up.

"What's wrong with your penis?"

"Nothing. My depression meds just make it kinda numb."

"Then you're gonna stop taking them. Tomorrow we'll pick up where we left off."

"Okay."

We got dressed and went to class. I skipped my meds that night. Tanya came over the next day. She was wearing white sneakers and a purple spandex onesie. We went up to my room and closed the door. She stripped naked and got on her knees. She pulled down my pants and boxers and grabbed my cock. She looked up at me.

"I'm gonna suck him. And when you're close, I want you to pull out and cum all over my face."

I lost my breath. I nodded and closed my eyes. I felt an explosion of warmth. It was like she'd swallowed my entire body. She worked on me for a few minutes. Something inside me clicked. My legs shook. Then my whole skeleton jangled.

"Oh Jesus, I'm coming," I yelled.

I pulled myself from her mouth. She smiled and tilted her head back. Sperm gushed out of me. It covered her nose and cheeks and lips and chin. She opened her mouth and moaned. I moaned with her. The orgasm faded. I pinched the last drop on her teeth. She licked it off and stood. The mess slid down her face and dripped onto her tits and belly. She stuck out her tongue and walked to the bathroom. She lifted her hair and cocked her hip.

"Your cum looks good on me. But next time, I want more."

The blood drained from my face. I was hooked.

We spent the next three weeks ruining sheets. We made our relationship official at some point. We finished our finals and fucked to celebrate. As we lay sweaty in bed, Tanya turned to me.

"When do you leave?" she asked.

I'd planned a summer trip with three of my Livermore homies to Central America—Cancún to Costa Rica for six weeks. It was gonna be an epic adventure. I couldn't wait.

"August second."

She wrapped her leg around mine and laid her cheek on my chest.

"Good. Plenty of time for you to meet Mommy and Daddy."

"Mommy and Daddy?"

"Yep. And then I'm meeting your mommy and daddy."

"Wonderful."

We packed that Saturday and split. We took my ride as Tanya was sans wheels. The plan was to visit her folks in Reseda.[135] We'd chill a few days, then I'd shoot up to my folks' in Livermore on my own. Tanya would catch a ride with a friend the last weekend in July. She'd meet my folks, then I'd drop her back off in Reseda and continue to SD, where I'd catch a flight with my homies to Cancún.

We arrived in Reseda at sundown. We turned off the main drag and onto a shady lane. The trees along the sidewalk looked like tired giants; their branches swayed with syrupy motion. We passed rows and rows of eggshell houses with gray lawns. Tanya bobbed her head to the song "Float On."[136] I yawned and gripped the steering wheel. Tanya straightened her back.

"There my house be!" she said, pointing.

I looked over her finger. It landed on a yellow house with white trim. Its paint was peeling in polka dots. Its windows were cracked, and its roof was missing tiles. Its lawn was a cesspool of hose water and dead grass. Its driveway had a rainbow of oil stains and a beige Pinto with flat tires and a 76 ball[137] on its antenna. I pulled up next to the Pinto. Tanya squealed and flung open the door. She ran across the walkway and onto the porch. The screen door opened and out stepped an old man. He had a silver

---

[135] Neighborhood in the San Fernando Valley region of Los Angeles, California, founded in 1912, was devoted to agriculture for many years. Parts of the neighborhood have been used in major films such as *The Karate Kid, Terminator II, Boogie Nights,* and *Erin Brockovich.*

[136] Song by boredom-inducing American indie rock band Modest Mouse. It was released on March 8, 2004, as the lead single from their fourth godawful studio album, *Good News for People Who Love Bad News* (2004). The song unfortunately topped the US Billboard Modern Rock Tracks chart and was nominated for a Grammy Award for Best Rock Song in 2005. The music video is portrayed in the style of a pop-up book with the band wearing turn-of-the-century clothing and dildos for noses.

[137] Styrofoam antenna balls created in 1967 by Union Oil as an homage to their 76 gasoline, which references the 1776 United States Declaration of Independence. The balls were especially popular in the Greater Los Angeles area, where they are still seen today.

afro and a gunmetal mustache. A pair of hornrims[138] rested on his elbow-sized nose. He wore blue jeans with faded knees and a short-sleeved collared. His arms were scrawny and his gut was a wad of dough. He donned a withered smile when he saw Tanya. She threw her arms around him and squeezed.

"Daddy," she cried.

His hornrims almost popped off. He chuckled and pushed them back on his schnoz. The screen door opened again. This time a woman stepped out. She was the size of a small hippo. She wore a black kimono and a braid down her back. Her nose was flat and her eyes were pinched. She had tiny hands and giant forearms. Tanya unclasped herself from her father and faced the woman.

"Hi, Mommy," she said.

The woman grinned. Her teeth were ivory squares. She hugged her daughter with one arm. Tanya hugged her back then motioned me over. I clicked off the ignition and frowned.

"Here we go," I muttered.

I got out of the car and forced a smile. Tanya bounced to attention.

"Johann, this is my daddy, Marshall."

"Hiya," he said to me.

"And this is my mommy, Lidia."

"Hola Juancito," she said. "When are dju gonna marry my bootiful daughter?"

I almost choked. Lidia broke into a furious cackle. She reached out and flicked my belly button.

"I only *keed* you," she said.

I bunched my lips and nodded. The four of us went inside. Footsteps pounded down the hall. They sounded like a derailing freight train. Three women entered the

---

[138] Type of eyeglasses, originally made of either horn or tortoise shell; however, for most of their history they have been constructed out of thick plastics designed to imitate those materials.

anteroom. Two were young and one was old. The youngest was morbidly obese with black hair and dark skin. The next-to-youngest was slightly less obese with lighter features. The older woman had brown hair and a tan complexion. Amazingly, she was but plump.

"Johann, these are my sisters, Mia and Alejandra," Tanya said, pointing to the girls. "And this is my granny, Alma." She pointed to the older woman.

I simpered and shook their hands. My skin started to itch. I raised my eyebrows like, "Is that all of 'em?" Tanya gave me a dirty look. I heard the pattering of feet. I thought it might be a cat. An ancient woman entered the room. She was hunched and wrinkled and gray. A ratty white braid ran down her back. She wore a yellow shawl over a blue jacket over a green nightgown. Her ankles were swollen and purple and stuffed into a pair of threadbare slippers. She had the face and eyes of a dried mackerel. She raised a crumpled fist to her lips and coughed. Tanya flushed with happiness.

"And this," she said proudly, "is our dear, sweet matriarch Great Gramma Guadeloupe."

"*Encantado de conocerle,*" I said, extending my hand. Pleased to meet you.

Triple-G stared me in the face. I became conscious of my lip piercing. She reached out and touched it with her spitty finger. I jumped back.

"*¡Demonio!*" she shouted.

Tanya put her hands on Triple-G's shoulders.

"*Cálmese,*" she said. "*El es mi novio, no un demonio.*" He is my boyfriend, not a demon.

"*¡No! ¡Es un maldito demonio!*" No! He's a damn demon!

Lidia stepped in. She grabbed her grandmother by the forearm and led her down the hall. Triple-G got smaller and smaller—like God had wrapped his clear hand around her and squeezed her into a prune. Tanya took a deep breath and shook her mane out. Then she turned to me.

"Don't worry. Great Gramma threw chicken blood on Danny the first time she met him."

"Where the hell did she get that?"

She pointed her finger to the sliding glass door across the house. I looked and saw five white chickens. Four were picking at trash on the grass. One was kicking around in a kale-colored swimming pool. The scene made me acutely aware of my surroundings. I turned at the threshold and soaked it in. The anteroom was a smoke den of moth-eaten couches and orange walls. The hall was a dark corridor of religious artifacts and melted candles. The kitchen was a bit of everything: mounds of dishes, piles of paper, stacks of pots and pans, old phonebooks in small towers, vases with dead flowers, spice racks, mud tracks, and twenty kinds of dust. I saw a series of animal cages. Tanya introduced the inhabitants of each.

"These are our four guinea pigs, and our three cockatiels, and our two bunny rabbits, and our turtle named Sam."

"Did Triple-G ritually sacrifice the partridge?"

"We also have two cats, Emily and Silvia. But who knows where they are."

"Great. Let's unpack."

She led me to the guestroom. It was a dinky space with pink walls and a half bath. I noticed the single bed. I looked at Tanya and frowned.

"We're not sleeping together?"

"No darlin'. I sleep in my bedroom with Great Gramma."

The thought of sleeping next to that wizened extraterrestrial made me shudder. I plopped my bags on the ground and sighed. Tanya slid her hand around my crotch.

"Don't worry," she whispered. "We'll get some alone time."

I spent the night tossing and turning. I tried to jerk off in the bathroom sink but it was impossible to maintain an erection with Triple-G wheezing in the next room. I passed out from exhaustion at 4:00 a.m. I woke up to the sound of screaming in the kitchen. I put my ear to the door. I heard Lidia say, "Do what you're told" in Spanish, then Tanya fired back with, "I'm a grown woman, you can't force me." Silence ensued. I ran to my bed and pulled the sheet over my legs. Tanya opened the door and closed it behind her. Her eyes were beet red.

"You have a good night's sleep, hon?" she asked.

"Not really."

"Up thinkin' about me?"

"More or less."

"Awww, I know what you need."

She walked toward me. Her hips swayed like a candle flame. She stopped at the bed and pulled my sheets back. I'd pitched a tent in my boxers.

"Looks like someone's happy to see me."

I nodded pitifully. She took me by the hand and into the bathroom. She closed the door and pulled off her jeans. She was wearing pink ankle socks but no panties. Her pussy was stubbly. It smelled like strawberry lotion and baked beans. I lifted her onto the sink and stood between her legs. I gripped her wide hips and sunk my dick in. The pleasure was immense. It felt like a water tower of smack being pushed into my vein. I flitted my eyes and pumped. Tanya gripped the bottom of the sink with one hand and fingered her clit with the other. We clapped and clapped. The walls shook and the mirror flapped. Tanya opened her mouth to scream. Her pussy tightened around my cock.

"I'm coming," she mouthed.

I grinned wide. I spit on my fingers and massaged her clit. She dropped her arms and threw her head back. Her body electrocuted itself on my dick. I stood and watched the show. When it ended, she looked at me.

"That was nice. But next time, keep thrusting while I'm coming. Makes it more intense."

"Oh." I dropped my shoulders and undocked. Tanya plucked some tissues and wiped her pussy. She bounced off the sink and looked down. My dick was still hard.

"You didn't cum?"

"No."

"And I suppose you want me to suck it outta you."

"Uh-huh."

"Fine. But I want you to know that you're very spoiled."

I smiled and shrugged. She got on her knees and sucked. My joints loosened in unison. I felt like a wax skeleton being burned at the stake. It took a single minute. I pulled my cock out and held it to her tongue. She grinned and tilted her chin. Streaks of cum raced out and filled the back of her throat. One missed its mark and shot across her cheek. I finished and took away my cock. She swiped the pearly streak with her middle finger and licked it. She swallowed my entire load. I collapsed on my heels. She stood and grabbed her pants.

"Clean up and come to the kitchen. Gramma and I are making *pupusas*."[139]

I washed my junk and got dressed. I came out twenty minutes later. Alma was pounding masa in a metal bowl. Tanya was grating cheese, while chicharrones sizzled on the stove. The smell was terrific. A big card table was in the middle of the kitchen. I grabbed a plastic chair and

---

[139] Thick griddle cake or flatbread from El Salvador and Honduras made with *masa* (cornmeal) or rice flour. In El Salvador, it has been declared the national dish and has a specific day to celebrate it called *Día Nacional de la Pupusa* ("National Pupusa Day"), which is on November 8th. Pupusas are usually stuffed with one or more ingredients, which may include cheese, *chicharrón* (fried pork belly), squash, or refried beans. They are typically accompanied by *curtido* (a spicy cabbage slaw) and *salsa roja* (tomato salsa) and are traditionally eaten by hand.

sat. People filtered in and joined me. Tanya and Alma plated dinner. They served three stacks of pupusas, home-made salsa roja, and curtido. Hands flew at the food. The kitchen filled with the sounds of clinking, clanking, and chewing. Nobody said a word. I could sense lingering tension between Tanya and her mother. I ignored it and ate. Lidia looked at her daughter then at me.

"So Juancito. How dju and my daughter meet?"

Tanya huffed. I forced a smile and told the story. Lidia listened to the end. She flicked her eyes skyward and grinned.

"Oh, dju reminding me of how I met to Marshall."

"Oh yeah?"

"Siiiii, it all khappen when I was eighteen."

She recounted how she'd been a cashier at a fast-food joint called The Finger-Lickin' Chicken. She said Marshall was the owner and that he took a liking to her right away. She recalled how good-looking he'd been at fifty, that he'd had less gray hair and wrinkles. She said she considered herself lucky to meet such a *gringo caballero.*[140] That is, of course, until his business flopped.

"Stupid *pendejo*[141] didn't got tha brains to pay khis loans. Khee loos everything, but what can I do? I fresh off tha boat from El Salvador and already pregnant wit Tanya. We must to get married."

I looked at Marshall. He was staring blankly at his pupusa. Lidia was now describing what an *idiota* he'd been at their wedding. All the ladies, except Tanya, were laughing. The whole scene was nauseating. I tossed my napkin on the table and stood.

"Thanks for the lovely meal, Lidia."

---

[140] Spanish term meaning foreign gentleman, white American gentleman, or whiteboy gentleman. It isn't necessarily offensive, but it can be.

[141] Spanish slang word meaning idiot or dumbass. Its literal translation is pubic hair, and it was originally used to describe pubescent teens who behaved foolishly.

She pressed her face into a cutesy smile.

"Djor very welcome, Juancito."

I went to my room and closed the door. I put on *The College Dropout*[142] and chilled. I heard screaming through the music. I removed my headphones and listened. Tanya and her mother were at it again. I couldn't catch everything, but I was sure it had something to do with what had transpired at the dinner table. Spanish curse words were tossed back and forth. Tanya shouted, "I hate you," then pounded down the hall. She opened her door and slammed it. I heard bedsprings squeak. I waited ten minutes. I got up, washed my face, and went over there. I heard her crying. I twisted the knob and pushed open the door. Tanya was sitting on her bed. Half of her hair was down her back, the other half dangling over her lap. Her right fist was balled against her left shoulder. She was gripping a knife and slicing her flesh. Blood gushed down her arm. I bolted into the room and grabbed her wrist. She pulled back with surprising strength. I shook the knife from her hand and bear-hugged her. She kicked and screamed. I put my mouth to her ear.

"Stop it," I whispered.

She went limp. I loosened my grip and we sat for a minute. I unlocked my arms from her chest and grabbed some Kleenex. I cleaned myself and handed her the box. She took it and plucked a dozen tissues. She blew her nose

---

[142] Debut studio album by American rapper and producer Kanye West. It was released on February 10, 2004, by Roc-A-Fella Records and Def Jam Recordings. The album showcased Kanye's "chipmunk soul" musical style, which made use of sped up, pitch shifted vocal samples from soul and R&B records. It also featured the artist's own drum programming, string accompaniments, and gospel choirs. Diverging from the then-dominant gangster-related themes in hip hop, West's lyrics concern organized religion, family, sexuality, excessive materialism, self-consciousness, minimum wage labor, institutional prejudice, and personal struggles. The album was promoted with singles such as "Through the Wire," "Jesus Walks," "All Falls Down," and "Slow Jamz." To date, it has sold over four million copies.

with blood still running down her arm. She wadded the tissues and held them to her cut. I chuckled and pulled her hair around her ears. I rubbed her back in circles. She dropped her head and cried again.

"That fucking bitch," she said, miserably. "She knows damn well it's her fault that Daddy defaulted on his loans. She's always blowing the money he makes on phones and clothes and lotto tickets. Then she has the audacity to mock him in front of everyone."

I didn't know what to say. She stood, grabbed the knife, and slipped it into her nightstand drawer. She took an elbow-sleeved top from the closet and went into her bathroom. I heard the sink run and the toilet flush. She came out a minute later wearing the top. Her arm was clean and a big dinosaur Band-Aid was on her wound. She pulled her sleeve over the Band-Aid and pinned her hair up. She looked at me and grinned.

"Wanna watch Newsies?"[143] she asked.

"Sure."

I left the next morning after a tremendous bout of bathroom sex. I was supposed to stay another day, but I made the excuse that my mother missed me. I blasted rap the whole way to Livermore. It soothed my nerves after all the emo, pop, and musicals.

I pulled in front of our two-story white McMansion[144]

---

[143] 1992 American musical historical drama film produced by Walt Disney Pictures. Loosely based on the New York City newsboys' strike of 1899, it stars Christian Bale, Bill Pullman, Ann Margret, and Robert Duvall. The film was an initial box office bomb, which was well-deserved. It later gained a cult following on home video and was adapted into a gag-worthy stage piece on Broadway. The play was nominated for eight Bologna Awards, winning two, including Best Original Bore.

[144] Pejorative term for a large, mass-produced, upper-middle class suburban home, which prizes superficial appearance and sheer size over quality.

at sundown. I walked across our manicured lawn and up our slate steps. I keyed our heavy door and opened it. The smell of enchiladas and beans filled my nose. My Mexican grandparents, Nina and Papito, were visiting. They sat at the kitchen table, chatting. Nina was wearing black capris and a big green sweater. Her hair was braided and clipped into a spiral around her head. Papito was in his black Dickies and matching collared. His white hair was combed to one side and his reading glasses rested low on his nose. My father was in his gray sweatpants and T-shirt. He was stretched out in his La-Z-Boy like a sunbathing grizzly, scratching his beard and watching TV. Our dog Buffster was on her little bed in front of the sliding glass door. My mom was walking back and forth in her blue apron and white summer dress, serving plates and humming the oldies on the radio. I dragged my bags across the hardwood walkway and into the kitchen. Everyone turned and smiled.

"Hey bud, how'd it go?" my mom asked.

"Interesting, to say the least."

I went upstairs and dumped my crap. I came back down, hugged everyone, and sat. Dinner looked delicious. I slathered it in *chile verde*[145] and guacamole and dug in. Between chomps, I explained the finer points of my stay with Tanya and Co. I left out the more graphic parts, but I gave enough to paint a vivid picture. My folks were shocked silent. Nina smiled and nodded. Papito looked around, clueless.

"*¿Qué dice?*" he said, fixing his hearing aid. What's he saying?

---

[145] Spanish for green chili, often refers to a spicy New Mexican stew made from chunks of pork that have been slow cooked in chicken broth, garlic, green tomatillos, and roasted green chilis. However, in my family, it refers to a super spicy green chili salsa made from jalapeños, habaneros, garlic, cumin, oregano, and other ingredients. The recipe was handed down by my great grandmother, who was originally from San Luis Potosí, Mexico.

Nina leaned in and shouted the abridged Spanish version into his ear. He grumbled loudly and raised his eyebrows.

"And you say she's Mexican?" he asked in Spanish.

"No Papito," I yelled. "She's half Salvadorian."

"I see. And what's the other half?"

"Russian Jew."

His face warped.

"Los pinches judíos no valen verga," he spat. The fuckin' Jews ain't worth dick.

"Anyways," I said to the rest of the table, "she'll be here in four weeks."

"You know the rules," my mother said.

"Are you fucking kidding me? I'm twenty-two and I've been around the world five times. You mean to tell me I can't sleep in the same room with my girl?"

"Not if you're not married."

"Whatever. I'll figure something else out."

I finished my dinner and went upstairs. I got on the horn with my buddy Tim. I explained the situation.

"That's *bitchin'*,"[146] he said.

"Tell me about it."

I asked if his younger brother Sebastian was still living in the pool house.

"Yeah, but he's camping with his buddies that weekend. I'm sure he'll let you and Tanya use it if you drop him a few bones."

"Seezly?"[147]

"Chea hea. Hit him up."

He gave me Sebastian's number. I called him and got the okay. I texted Tanya the good news. She texted back: "Yippee. I'll bring my lingerie."

---

[146] Of inferior quality; not all that great; silly; ridiculous.

[147] Seriously?; You've gotta be kidding me!

Over the next six weeks, I was a fiend. When I wasn't drinking to excess with my homies and fantasizing about our trip to Central America, I was in my bedroom with a bottle of lotion, rubbing one out to thoughts of Tanya. I must've jerked off three times a day. The toilet paper I used for clean-up could've filled an entire dumpster. I grew visibly thinner. I covered it by wearing baggy flannels.

My sister Hannah arrived the last Friday in July to celebrate her birthday. She was wearing a yellow "Cal" T-shirt and carrying a duffle bag with the word Berkeley on it. I greeted her at the front door and said, "Happy Birthday." She hugged me then stood back.

"You look skinny," she said.

I pulled at the ends of my flannel.

"Nah, this thing is just kinda big on me."

"Uh-huh."

She fixed her curls and walked into the kitchen. She greeted our parents and grandparents and pet Buffster. Everyone told her "Happy Birthday" and gave her hugs. My dad brought out presents and my mom showed her the cake. My phone vibrated in my pocket. I pulled it out and saw a text from Tanya: "I'm here :)"

I excused myself and went out front. I saw a blue VW Bug across the street. I recognized the driver as one of Tanya's girlfriends. She honked and waved and sped away. I turned and faced the sidewalk. Tanya was at the end of our stone walkway with her suitcase by her side. She was dressed in a purple miniskirt and tube top. She wore fishnet stockings and black leather boots with stiletto heels. She thinned her dark little eyes. Her heels made the sound of bones snapping as she walked. My body went limp around my swollen cock. She reached out and put her hand on my crotch.

"Miss me?" she whispered in my ear.

I let out a tiny breath. She squeezed my shaft and released it. I stuck her suitcase in my trunk. I went into the house and walked her to the kitchen. Everyone was at the table, chatting. They fell silent when they saw Tanya. I gulped and introduced her. Nobody uttered a word for ten seconds.

"Welcome," my mother finally said.

We had an awkward lunch and an even more awkward dinner. My sister blew out her candles and opened presents, and Tanya said but five words. Every so often she pinched my leg or flicked her tongue at me. It was sexy at first, but it soon became annoying. I caught my granny eyeballing her after we'd had cake. I stood and clapped my hands.

"Welp, it's time we got going."

Tanya looked relieved. She said goodbye and went to my car. I stuffed some clothes in a bag and made for the door. My mother stopped me.

"Are you really gonna sleep at the Frazelli's pool house on your sister's birthday?"

I bent my mouth into an arch.

"This isn't my doing."

That night, Tanya did a striptease for me to the song "Teardrop."[148] We fucked afterwards and I came on her face. As she was wiping up, she gave me a funny look. I pulled my boxers on and jumped in bed.

"What?" I asked.

She threw the wad of toilet paper on the floor and climbed in next to me.

"Are you ever going to cum inside me?"

My skin tightened around my ribcage like a straitjacket.

"Is it really that important?"

"Well, yeah. We don't have to do it every time, but

---

[148] Song by English trip hop group Massive Attack. It was released as the second single from the group's third studio album, *Mezzanine*, on April 27, 1998. In the UK, the song peaked at number 10.

sometimes would be nice."

"You're not on the pill."

"So?"

"Whaddaya mean, 'So'?"

"Danny came inside me all the time and I wasn't on the pill. I never got pregnant. We just timed it right."

"First off, I don't wanna fucking hear about Danny coming inside you. Second, 'You just timed it right'? Do you know how ridiculous that sounds?"

"It's not ridiculous; it worked fine for two years. I know my body, Johann."

"Yeah, but you don't know my jizz. It might be supercharged or something."

She glared at me.

"I know your jizz, stupid."

"Haha. Not inside you, you don't."

"Can't we try it? I can take the morning after pill if you're really that worried."

I folded my hands over my belly button and stared at them.

"It's not just about you getting pregnant."

"Oh?" she replied, sitting up.

"No. For me, coming inside a woman means something."

"Okay, what's it mean?"

"It means I'm in love with her."

She bent forward and laughed.

"Good Lord, you're a sensitive boy."

"I knew you'd make fun of me."

"Oh, come on. I was kidding. Don't you think it means something that I'm asking you to cum inside me? Don't you think I love you too?"

The word slapped me across the face.

"You love me?"

"I'm trying to."

"I'm also trying to. But I gotta be honest, I'm not quite there yet."

She covered her teeth and dropped her head. I felt a pang of guilt. I put my hand on her knee and rubbed it.

"Let's see what happens tomorrow night."

"Okay," she said, sniffling.

The next day we had the second phase of Hannah's twentieth. My mother invited both sides of the family and cooked a feast. Things were less awkward with Tanya, partly because she wore a less provocative outfit and partly because she made fast friends with my younger cousins. She played hide-and-seek with them upstairs. Then she took them to the backyard to play soccer. I watched from the kitchen window and poured a drink. I went to the snack table and grabbed some cashews. My grandmother Nina sat on the adjacent couch. She waved me over.

"What's up, Neen?" I said, sitting next to her.

She bit her cookie and brushed the crumbs off her blouse.

"So, tell me," she said, chewing, "How are things with you and your little girlfriend?"

"Pretty good. We've been going together for about two months. I think we have a chance."

"At what?"

"A strong relationship."

Her cheery face turned serious. She raised her long-nailed finger and tipped it.

"Uh-uh. Girls like her don't make strong relationships; they only make problems. Do yourself a favor and guard your heart."

"But we're already going together. I can't break it off."

"I didn't say break it off," she said, tapping my knee. "You can have your fun. And you should; you're young. I'm just saying be careful. Because after what I've seen and what you've told me about her family, it seems like one big trap."

I thanked her for the advice and necked my drink. I poured myself another and proceeded to get drunk. We had dinner and watched Hannah open more presents. We ate cake, then people left. I was hammered at this point. Tanya had had a few sips of booze but she was okay to drive. My mother refused to let us leave. She said if we promised to sleep with separate blankets, we could stay. We crossed our hearts and went up to my room. We immediately got naked and fucked. We went from the bed to the bathroom to the floor. Tanya straddled me and rode me like a horse. She rubbed her clit and made herself cum. Then she focused on me. She gyrated her hips and bounced her ass. I lay flat and drooled. I felt the tingle of an orgasm. It rushed up on me like a crook. I gripped the carpet and moaned. Tanya moaned with me. She squeezed off my load and collapsed on my chest.

"That was awesome," she said, panting.

I realized what I'd done. I pushed her off and crawled on the bed. I hugged my legs and stuck my chin between my knees. Tanya stood and glared at me.

"What's wrong?" she asked.

"Nothing."

"Then why are you acting weird?"

"Because."

"Because why?"

"Because . . . I don't know . . . Like, what if you're pregnant now?"

"Oh my God, we just had the best sex of our relationship and that's all you can think about?"

"How can I *not* think about it? You forced me to cum inside you."

"Forced you? What the hell are you implying?"

"I don't know. Maybe you did this on purpose. Maybe you want to get pregnant."

"Good Lord. I'm nineteen years old. Why the hell would I want to get pregnant?"

"Maybe it's not just you. Maybe someone else wants it too."

"Like who, my mother?"

"Maybe. She did make that comment about us getting married."

"She was joking."

"Didn't sound like it."

"You don't know what you're talking about."

She sat on my bed and hung her head. Tears ran down her cheeks. Guilt weighed in my stomach. I got up and handed her a roll of toilet paper. She ripped off a few sheets and blew her nose. She crumpled the snotty sheets into a wad and stuffed it into the cardboard roll.

"I wanted your first time to be something special. But you've ruined it, Johann. Ruined it with your paranoia and accusations. And what's worse, you're leaving on Monday for six weeks."

She sunk her face in her palms and sobbed. My blood turned yellow and my heart gushed. I felt like the rottenest cocksucker this side of Jupiter. I put my hand on her shoulder and rubbed.

"I'm just scared."

"Why?" she said, sniffing.

"Because . . . I think I'm in love with you."

"Really?"

"Yes."

"Then say it."

I opened my mouth. The words came out like zombie limbs from a grave.

"I love you, Tanya."

"I love you too, Johann."

I woke up the next morning with a splitting hangover. I fucked Tanya in the shower then packed my things. I called my buddies Bert, Mason, and Tim. We went over the logistics of our flight to Cancún. I said goodbye to my family and loaded my trunk. I got in the car with Tanya and away we sped. We arrived in Reseda six hours later. I drove to her house and parked. She looked at me and reached into her bag. She pulled out a letter and a hand-knit beanie.

"These are for you."

I was speechless. I took the items and smiled.

"Thank you."

"Welcome, lover. Don't open the letter until you get there."

I kissed her on the lips.

"I won't."

PART TWO

On the plane to Cancún, we each popped two Xanies[149] and washed 'em down with whiskeys. We slept the whole way. We landed and took a cab to Playa Tortugas.[150] We found a cheap room with four beds and a balcony overlooking the beach. We ate a meal of cat-crap tacos and bought some booze. My buddies went back to the room while I called Tanya. I told her we were having a blast. She feigned glee, but underneath I knew she was sad. I told her I'd call her again soon. We hung up, and I went back to the hotel to drink. This turned into a night at Señor Frog's.[151] I tried to have a good time and flirt with girls, but all I could think about was Tanya. I remembered her letter. I left the club and went on a long drunken walk back to our place. I found Tim and Mason hooking up with two local chicks. I ignored them and locked myself in the bathroom. I sat on the toilet and pulled out Tanya's letter. I unfurled its wrinkly yellow pages and read. The alcohol churned my emotions. As she slowly conveyed her love for me, my defenses crumbled. Tears rained down my cheeks. An orgasm of sadness blasted through my veins. I folded the letter and stuffed it back in my pocket. I washed my face, curled up in my bed, and drifted to sleep.

I woke up the next morning feeling like I'd been skull-fucked by He-Man. I went to Donald's with my homies and got Big Macs. I watched as Tim ran outside and vomited his food on the sidewalk. I went back to the room and spent the rest of the day lounging. Tim and Mason went

---

[149] American slang for Xanax.

[150] Touristy public beach in Cancún.

[151] Famous Cancún restaurant by day and a club by night. As a club, it hosts Conga lines, glow and foam parties, reggae sets, Latin dance shows, live bands, and wet T-shirt contests. Its motto is "Saving the world from boredom," and its mascot is an anthropomorphized frog wearing a pair of board shorts, a white T-shirt, a coral necklace, and a fedora.

out at night to bang their new squeezes. Bert hunted for one of his own, and I slept. I had a very odd dream. It started with me and my dawgz atop a famous cliffside restaurant on the Gulf of Mexico. The weather was chilly and it looked as if a storm was brewing. A blond waitress ushered us to a booth inside and took our orders. As she walked away, actor Seth Green[152] came and sat next to me. I was excited, but I chatted with him casually. I noticed a pustule forming on his left cheek. It grew into a soggy white pancake. I asked him what the hell it was. "Oh, this?" he replied. He sunk his fingers into his face and pulled out chunks of rotting flesh. I shrieked and left the restaurant. The wind was blowing furiously outside. It picked me up by the hips and spun me around. My arms flew backward, and two nails pierced my palms. I was pinned to a wooden cross that spiraled into a chasm. As I hit bottom, I awoke. My sense of reality was shaken, and I was on the verge of a panic attack. I needed something to calm my nerves. I got up and went for a stroll on the beach. Clear waves crashed along the shore. Rays of sunlight pierced the wall of clouds on the horizon. I knew the source of my anxiety. I missed Tanya terribly, or at least the idea of her. I sat on the sand and penned these words in my journal:

I might deserve a wonderful woman like her, but just barely. This is because I know she can grow from my experiences as I can grow from hers. If that were absent, I would pale like dying skin in her presence.

I went back to the room and showered. We took the

---

[152] American actor, producer, writer, and director (born February 8, 1974). Known as the most frequent voice on Adult Swim's *Robot Chicken* and as Doctor Evil's son "Scott Evil" in the *Austin Powers* film series. In 2004, he appeared in the comedy film *Without a Paddle*, which tells the story of three reunited childhood friends going on a trip up a remote river to search for the loot of long-lost airplane hijacker D. B. Cooper.

seven-forty bus to Chichén Itzá.[153] We wandered around the stone ziggurats for an hour. We filmed Mortal Kombat scenes in the jungle, ate, then took a bus to *El Centro*.[154] We got a cheap room at a new hotel. We had dinner, then I went to a phone house and called Tanya. She sounded better but still melancholy. I told her of my desire to remain faithful on the trip, and that my penis would only function sexually for her. She squealed with joy. We said I-love-you's and hung up. I walked back to the room and gathered my cronies. We went to a Cuban club called *El Gran Malao*. We got a table near the bar. We ordered beers and a round of shots. Mason spotted a hot chick and asked her to dance. I sat back and watched.

The next day, we took a bus headed south. We snored through our stop in Tulum[155] and got off in a sleepy little

---

[153] Pre-Columbian city built between 750 and 900 A.D. by the Maya people in Yucatán state, Mexico. It was one of the largest Maya cities and may have had the most diverse population in the Maya world. The Maya name Chichén Itzá means "At the mouth of the well of the Itzá"—the name of an ethnic-lineage group that gained political dominance in the region. Some of the site's most notable features are its cenotes (sinkholes), which contain the remains of human sacrifices, and its thirteen ballcourts for playing the Mesoamerican ballgame known as "Pitz" in the Maya language. According to some researchers, the game may have served to resolve conflicts without warfare. However, according to our tour guide, Pitz was a game played by warriors, in which the winner was given the honor of being decapitated at dusk, so his soul could follow the sun and protect it from demons as it descended into the spiritual underworld—an effort that would ensure a sunrise the next morning.

[154] Downtown area of Cancún. Unlike the tourist-ridden hotel zone located a few miles away, El Centro is a "locals only" area with authentic Mexican restaurants, bullfighting areas, quaint plazas, patches of Mayan ruins, and little dive bars hosting Latino music bands.

[155] Pre-Columbian Mayan walled city in the Mexican state of Quintana Roo. The ruins are situated on 12-meter (39 ft) tall cliffs along the east coast of the Yucatán Peninsula. The city was one of the last built and inhabited by the Maya; it was at its height between the 13th and 15th centuries and managed to survive about 70 years after the start of the Spanish conquest. Tulum is one of the best-preserved coastal Mayan cities and is the third most-visited archeological site in Mexico after Teotihuacán and Chichén Itzá.

town called Felipe Carrillo Puerto.[156] We ate Hawaiian pizzas and farted around the main square. We caught the five-forty bus to Chetumal[157] and arrived at 8:00 p.m. We took a cab to a skeezy hotel on the outskirts. The receptionist was a sweating ghoul with one gold tooth. He gave us a room on the second floor. It had two stained mattresses, fly-speckled walls, and a shitter from a boiler room nightmare.

We dumped our bags and went to Chez Mac.[158] We got nuggets and burgers and ate them in the back. We split and looked for a club to party at. Everything was boarded up or dead. I contemplated calling Tanya. I figured I'd wait till we got to the Belizean Cays.[159] We went back to the hotel. As we walked up the stairs, we saw our door was ajar. We pushed it open and looked inside. Our bags had been knifed and our clothes were strewn across the floor. We immediately took inventory. The thieves had stolen a silver necklace from me, sixty bucks from Bert, a tape recorder from Tim, and dirty sandals from Mason. We laughed at the silliness of it. We fixed our bags and the

---

[156] Municipal seat and largest city in Felipe Carrillo Puerto Municipality in Quintana Roo. In 2010, its population was 25,744 persons, mostly of Maya descent. The city was founded in 1850 by independent Maya under the name "Chan Santa Cruz." After it was conquered by Mexican troops in 1901, it was renamed "Santa Cruz del Bravo" before acquiring its present name—an homage to Felipe Carrillo Puerto (November 8, 1874 – January 3, 1924), a Mexican journalist, politician and revolutionary, who became known for his efforts at reconciliation after the Caste War (1847–1901)—a conflict that began with the revolt of native Maya people of the Yucatán Peninsula against Hispanic populations, called *Yucatecos*.

[157] City of 169,028 people (2020) on the east coast of the Yucatán Peninsula. It is the capital of the state of Quintana Roo and operates as Mexico's main trading gateway with neighboring Belize.

[158] Abbreviation of the term Chez MacDo, which is French slang for McDonald's.

[159] Collection of 450 cays on the Belize Barrier Reef—a 300-kilometer (190 mi) long section of the 900-kilometer (560 mi) Mesoamerican Barrier Reef System—which is continuous from Cancún down to Honduras, making it the second largest coral reef system in the world after the Great Barrier Reef in Australia.

paranoia set in. We grabbed our pocketknives and barri-
caded the doors and windows. We turned up the box
television super loud and played music and shouted. We
figured the ghoulish receptionist had orchestrated the
robbery. We waited till sunrise and got our revenge. We
stabbed the pillows and mattresses and spit on the walls.
We took out our dicks and pissed on the floors, then
dropped our drawers and left upper deckers in the toilet
tank. I had the number of the cabby who'd driven us to
the hotel. I called the fucker, and he picked us up lickety-
split and whisked us to the bus station. We cackled the
whole way. We got street tacos for breaky and took the
eleven forty-five to Belize City.[160]

It was a ride to beat the band. The sun was hot and
shiny, the sky was royal blue, and the jungle was a giant,
steaming mess of birds and trees and flowers. The little
dirt road was hell on our bones. Our cabin shook our crew
like dice in a plastic cup. We had every kinda fool on
board: pink-faced Mennonites[161] with wide straw hats and

---

[160] Largest city (pop. 57,169, in 2010) and principal port in Belize—
formerly known as British Honduras. It was founded as Belize Town in
1638 by English lumber harvesters. The location was ideal because it
was on a natural seaside outlet for local rivers down which logwood and
mahogany were shipped. As the industry developed, thousands of
African slaves were brought in by the English (known as "the British,"
beginning in 1707). Belize Town was the seat of British local courts and
government officials until 1981, when Belize gained its independence.

[161] Mennonites in Belize form different religious bodies and come
from different ethnic backgrounds. Religiously, there are groups who
are conservative, while others have modernized. Of the 10,000 ethnic
Mennonites in Belize, most are Russian, who speak Plautdietsch (a Low
German dialect), and a few hundred are Old Order Mennonites, who
speak Pennsylvania German. According to *The New York Times*,
"Mennonites began moving to Belize in the late 1950s . . . to live in line
with their religious beliefs, including the separation of church and
state, pacifism, and sustainability, without interference . . . from the
government." Most Belizean Mennonites are easily identified by their
clothing; the women wear bonnets and long, brightly colored dresses,
while the men wear denim overalls, traditional suspenders, dark
trousers, and hats. They have their own schools, churches, and
financial institutions. Some more conservative groups use horse-drawn
buggies for transportation, as both motors and electricity are forbidden.

filthy nails, little brown Maya[162] with beady eyes and bowl cuts, and big, buff creole blokes with tiny ears and skin as black as a fruit bat. A girl amongst them caught my attention. She had coffee thighs, red nails, and brown eyes that could yank the paint off a Chevy. She told me her name was Chrissy. I tried to keep it casual, but she kept crossing her legs and zapping me with her gaze. Her goofy gay friend put his hands over her eyes and turned her away. Mason took this as a sign and moved in. He chatted her up and got her number. I consoled myself with thoughts of Tanya.

We arrived in Belize City an hour later. We ate a meal of beans and rice then took the 2:00 p.m. boat to San Pedro.[163] The water was bluer than a drug lord's swimming pool. We sliced through it and docked in under ninety minutes. We walked past a sparkly white beach and through a maze of multicolored shacks. We found a crummy hotel on stilts called Julio's and got two doubles for ten bucks a pop. We dropped our crap and consulted

---

[162] Ethnolinguistic group of Mesoamerican indigenous peoples, generally descended from those of the ancient Maya civilization and today inhabit southern Mexico, Guatemala, Belize, El Salvador, and Honduras. Maya is a modern collective term; however, it was not historically used by the indigenous populations themselves as they had their own traditions, cultures, and histories, and shared no common sense of identity or political unity. It is estimated that seven million Maya were living in the aforementioned areas at the start of the 21st century. Some are quite integrated into majority mestizo cultures, while others continue a more traditional life, often speaking a Mayan language as a mother tongue. The Maya are known for their brightly colored textiles that are woven into capes, shirts, blouses, and dresses. Their religion is Roman Catholicism combined with indigenous Maya beliefs.

[163] Town on the southern part of Ambergris Cay—the largest island in Belize. It had a population of 16,444 (2015) and is the largest settlement and only town on Ambergris. Its inhabitants are known as San Pedranos; most of them originally came from Mexico and speak Spanish, English, and a blend of Belizean Creole and Spanish called "Kitchen Spanish." Fishing is a town-wide mainstay, and it is said one is not a true San Pedrano if one doesn't know how to fish. The town was allegedly the inspiration for Madonna's song "La Isla Bonita," which begins with, "Last night I dreamt of San Pedro."

the nearest bar. We chilled with local Garifuna[164] dudes and chicks from the states and drank and drank. At midnight, we hit up a food stand for some chicken. Mason had a hankering for pussy, so he hit up *Los Tigres*, the only club in town. The rest of us ate and went back to the hotel. I made a note to email Tanya in the morning.

I got up and went to the internet café. I wrote Tanya that I would cut my trip two weeks short and fly back on August 30th. I asked her about life and told her not to hold back. I said I loved and missed her, and that I couldn't wait to see her.

I spent the rest of the day with the guys. We swam in the sea and rode bikes around the cay. At night, Tim and Mason met two girls from Orange Walk.[165] They went to

---

[164] Descendants of indigenous Kalinago (Carib Indians) and Afro-Caribbean people who lived on the Caribbean Island of Saint Vincent and speak Garifuna, an Arawakan language, and Vincentian Creole. They were historically known by the exonym "Black Caribs." According to some researchers, their ethnicity was formed in the 1500s when Afro-Caribbeans seeking to escape slavery fled their respective islands and settled on Saint Vincent, where they were taken in by the Carib Indians, who offered them protection, then later mixed with them. In 1627, the English arrived on Saint Vincent and started a landgrab. Over time, tensions arose between the English and the Black Caribs. This led to The First and Second Carib Wars, which were spearheaded by Black Carib chieftain and Vincentian national hero Joseph Chatoyer. A major military expedition by British General Ralph Abercromby was eventually successful in killing Chatoyer and defeating the Black Carib opposition in 1796. The British authorities then deported those Black Caribs with more African features – as they were considered the cause of the revolt – to the island of Roatán in Honduras. Meanwhile, the ones with higher Amerindian traits were allowed to remain on the island. More than 5,000 Black Caribs were deported, but only 2,500 survived the trip. This wasn't enough to maintain their population on the island, so they asked the Spanish authorities of Honduras for permission to live on land, which was granted in exchange for the men's service as soldiers. After settling, the Black Caribs spread to Belize, Guatemala, and Nicaragua. They became known as "Garifuna," which is an Africanized derivation of the word "Kalinago," meaning "Carib Indians."

[165] Fourth largest town in Belize, with a population of about 13,400 (2010). It is located 53 miles (85 km) north of Belize City. Despite its

Los Tigres while Bert did his solo thing. I cut back to the room to do some soul-searching. I pulled out a pen and paper and wrote a love letter to Tanya. What poured out of me was a load of Shakespearean sap that could have covered every pancake in Canada. I didn't just write bad poetry, I complimented her profusely, and scolded myself for having ever disrespected her. I ended the letter with this:

I remember the night I came inside you. After I went on my childish tirade, I was scared to say, "I love you." But these days apart have shown me the light. I'm in love with you, Tanya, and I can't wait to see how beautifully it develops.

I folded the letter and stuffed it in my pocket. I fell asleep in a half-drunken stupor.

I woke up to my buddies showering and cracking jokes. I decided to quit the gushing and do some dude stuff. We rented bikes and rode around the marshland. We spotted crocs and snakes and every type of bird. We stopped at a grove of palm trees. I got it in me to do some crazy Indian brave shit. I ripped off my shirt and stuck my knife in my teeth. I made my hands and feet into a V and shimmied up the stalk of the tallest tree. I arrived at the top and grabbed my blade. I cut off a coconut and sliced my hand in the process. I slid down and checked the wound. It was long and skinny and filled with blood. I sucked it dry and wrapped it with my T-shirt. I grabbed the coconut and held it high like a severed head. This charged my homies into action. One after another, they climbed the tree and sliced down coconuts.

We collected our spoils and hacked them open. We poured the milk into a community water bottle and passed

---

English name, its residents are primarily Spanish-speaking mestizos, who, because of their constant contact with Anglophones, speak a version of Spanish which contains a rhotic ("R-like") consonant similar to the one in English.

it around. We each took a pull—we were Comanche[166] warriors drinking blood from the heart of a freshly slaughtered bull. The feeling was immense. It swallowed our bodies and leaked into the sky. We stood panting in our sticky glory. It had us by the balls.

The rest of the day was a blur. I think we went grocery shopping and drank a bunch, but I can't be sure. I know Tim's Orange Walk girl rousted him for a fuck in the middle of the night. I remember laughing at the calamity then falling back asleep.

I woke up to the sounds of Tim moaning in the shower. I chuckled, slipped on my thongs, and walked to the internet café. I saw an email from Tanya sent two days prior. It started with Yay then unfurled into a long and winding ramble. She talked about how she'd been hit on a bunch of times while working a silver stand with her friend

---

166 Native American nation from the Great Plains of the present-day United States. The US government federally recognizes the Comanche people as the Comanche Nation, headquartered in Lawton, Oklahoma. The Comanche language is a Numic language of the Uto-Aztecan family. The Comanche became the dominant tribe on the southern Great Plains in the 18th and 19th centuries after they adopted (and mastered) the use of the horse from Spanish colonists in New Mexico. As European Americans encroached on their territory, the Comanche waged war on and raided their settlements. They took thousands of captives and incorporated them into Comanche society. Cynthia Ann Parker (October 28, 1827 – March 1871), also known as "Naduah" (Comanche: "Narua," meaning "someone found"), was one of these people. She was kidnapped in 1836, at nine years of age, by a Comanche war band which had attacked her family's settlement. The tribe adopted her, and she lived with them for 24 years, completely discarding her childhood culture and identity. She married a Comanche chieftain, Peta Nocona, and had three children with him, including the last free Comanche chief, Quanah Parker. At age 34, she was discovered and captured by Texas Rangers, whereafter she was returned against her will to her extended biological family. She spent the remaining 10 years of her life refusing to reassimilate before committing suicide by voluntary starvation.

on Venice Beach,[167] how Triple-G had chased the chickens around the yard with a broom, and how some dude with a dainty smile and a dragonfly pinned to his hat had tried to sell her E.[168] She spent a significant amount of time explaining her family's financial problems, how they dropped four G's a month on mortgage payments, and that it was no wonder her daddy had trouble covering her tuition.

I'll be having a glorious day, she wrote. *Then I'll suddenly remember we might lose the house, and I'll burst into tears. I wish I could sign for a stupid loan, but I don't have credit. None of my friends do either, and they're all too scared of my family.*

I could feel myself being pulled in a bad direction. This was exacerbated when she wrote that she'd called her ex, Danny, and bawled with him over the phone. She wondered why she had to get over him when she was the one who'd done the breaking up. She said she missed me, missed my arms, missed my touch. She apologized for stealing me away from my friends. She ended with, *I don't write emails often, but when I do, they're about the length of my hair.*

I pulled my face from the screen and blinked. I felt like I had been on a rollercoaster through the mind of an acid-

---

[167] Neighborhood of Los Angeles known for its canals, which inspired its name, and its beach, which receives millions of visitors a year. Venice Beach has been labeled as "a cultural hub known for its eccentricities." It includes Muscle Beach, the Venice Beach Recreation Center, a bike trail, and Ocean Front Walk—a promenade which runs parallel to the beach and is host to artists, performers, fortune-tellers, and vendors.

[168] American street slang for the drug (or mix thereof) called "ecstasy." Its primary ingredient is the psychoactive molecule 3,4-Methylenedioxymethamphetamine (MDMA), which causes altered sensations and increased energy, empathy, and feelings of sexual pleasure. "E" is commonly associated with dance parties, raves, and electronic dance music. It often comes in the form of a pressed pill, which contains MDMA, and may contain other substances such as ephedrine, amphetamine, and methamphetamine.

tripping nymph. I thought about the love letter I'd written her; I didn't have the time or strength to type it. I explained this in a short email. I told her I loved her dearly and that she was a strong woman.

I sent the email and went back to Julio's. I grabbed my shit and split with the boys on the one o'clock boat to Cay Caulker.[169] We arrived half an hour later. Caulker was smaller than Ambergris, with two roads and few hotels—we found one with a quad for thirty-five bucks. It had four single beds, a rusty AC, and a busted-ass TV. We dumped our crap and got food—six-dollar lobster burritos that looked like they had been consumed and regurgitated by a retarded infant. We bounced and looked for the Caulker equivalent of Los Tigres. We found it at the edge of a sandbar that melted into an estuary. We ordered Belikins[170] and cheers'd. The last thing I remember is watching some dude with leathery skin reel in a snapper.

The next day was snorkel day. We took a tour of the reef on a boat called the *Akista* and hit three different spots. We swam with nurse sharks, sea turtles, and stingrays. We drank beers on the deck and bullshitted with the guides. We got back and hit a rib joint. Our server was a slender Belizean woman with frizzy hair and tawny

---

[169] Small limestone coral island off the coast of Belize measuring about five miles (8.0 km) by less than one mile (1.6 km). Its population is approximately 2,000 and its town is known as Cay Caulker Village. The island is located approximately 20 miles (32 km) north-northeast of Belize City and is accessible by high-speed water taxi or small plane. It is thought to have been inhabited for hundreds of years; however, the recent population levels did not start until the Caste War of Yucatán in 1847, when many mestizos of mixed Maya and Spanish descent fled the massacres taking place across the Yucatán. The island has been ravaged by many hurricanes, the most notable of which were Hattie in 1961 and Keith in 2000. In recent years, it has become a popular destination for backpackers and other tourists.

[170] Leading domestically produced beer brand in Belize. It is brewed by the Belize Brewing Company, Ltd. (est. 1969), which is owned by the Bowen family and based in Ladyville, Belize District. The name Belikin comes from the Maya language and means "Route to the East"—a term which some have suggested is the origin of the name Belize.

skin. She had a round ass split in half by a white lace thong; the summer dress she had on was see-through. We gnawed our ribs and fantasized about that ass. We finished and I cut to check my email.

I already had three from Tanya. The first was simply titled "Prrrraaaaaa." It was paragraph after paragraph of her ranting—mostly about Triple-G, and her three best friends, Zulma, Amos, and Shoshi. The second was an inquiry as to whether I'd worn my beanie. The final started with, *I'm pathetic*, then described how two polite guys had come to see her house and she'd been dry and cynical toward them.

I used to be so sweet, she wrote. *But they were here to take my house. If only I had credit or knew someone who did. Oh well.*

Next came the part about Danny. She said she called him again to ask how he was doing and that the conversation "degraded into tears." I sensed there was more to the story. I got on AIM[171] and messaged her. She seemed distant at first. She soon spilled the beans. This time she had gone to Danny's house. They had a little talk and things got tense, so she gave him a back massage. He turned around and claimed he had an eyelash in his eye. She leaned forward to pluck it out and he went for the kiss. She said she resisted. *But we still cried in each other's arms*, she wrote.

Rage screamed through my system. It threatened to surge out my fingertips as I typed. I managed to gain control. I told her if her relationship with Danny continued, there would be major problems. She agreed to see much

---

[171] AOL Instant Messenger, an instant messaging and presence computer program created by AOL. It was popular from the late 1990s to the late 2000s in North America and was the leading instant messaging application in that region. Teens and college students were known to use the messenger's "away message" feature to keep in touch with friends and to inform them throughout the day of their ongoings, location, thoughts, and feelings.

less of him. I wanted to fire back with, *You shouldn't fucking see him at all,* but I refrained. We ended the conversation on a withered goodbye. I went to the john and washed my face. I came back, calm and composed. I remembered my love letter. I typed it and pressed Send. I felt a lot better.

I returned to the room and gathered the guys. We ate at a Belizean BBQ, then we rented rods and hit the dock. We sat at the edge and threw out our lines. I was the first to get a bite. I stood and reeled in my catch. I yanked it from the water and onto the dock. It was a baby nurse shark. It couldn't have weighed more than a few pounds. It sucked at the air and flopped around on its back. Its belly was flat and glowed white in the moonlight. I grabbed it by the gill and tried to remove the hook. It was lodged deep in its guts. I knew I couldn't remove it without killing the poor thing. I pulled out my knife and cut the line. I lifted the baby shark and held it above the water. It felt like I was carrying my own child. I kissed it on the snout and slid it into the sea. I had to imagine it swimming away because the water was too dark to see.

The next morning, we caught the eleven-thirty boat to Belize City. Our plan was to stay the night so Mason could bang Chrissy, the creole girl with the coffee thighs and striking brown eyes. We drove around the sweltering ghetto looking for a place. We failed to find one where the chances of having our throats slit were less than fifty-fifty. We got on a bus and booked it to San Ignacio,[172] a jungle town some twenty minutes from the border with

---

[172] Largest settlement in Cayo District (Western Belize) and the second largest in the country, with a population of 17,878 (2010). The town got its start from mahogany and chicle production during British colonization. Over time, it attracted Mestizo, Creole, Lebanese, Mopan Maya, Mennonite, and Chinese—most of whom emigrated from Guangzhou in the mid-20th century.

Guatemala. We spent the whole ride with our noses wedged into the stinky armpits of Mennonites. We arrived as the sun was dipping in the sky and shooting out orange rays that lit up the trees and the kaleidoscope of rooftops around the main square. We got off the bus and looked for a room. We found one for thirty bucks with four beds and a balcony overlooking a colorful thoroughfare. I dumped my crap and went to the nearest internet café. I was eager to see if Tanya had responded to my love letter. I logged onto AOL[173] and checked. Sure enough, she'd sent me four emails. I opened the one entitled "I need . . ." It read:

Sex. Lots of sex. I'm fucking horny. Grrrrrrrr. Oh, God. My vagina is throwing a fit. She is deprived. My libido is waking up and it is very unappreciated. This is unnecessary. Oh, and it's kinda funny. Zulma's drunken sex scorecard is 1 Irish guy and 1 Chinese girl. I wanna have sex with a girl. Fook. Does Amos count? He's kinda gay. Where can I find a girl to have sex with? I know you'd be ok with that. I can't find one. Shoshi prolly won't 'cuz she'd want a threesome with her bf and I don't. Grrrr. Sex.

My face turned the collective red of all the popped hymens in Persia. I clamped my hands around the monitor and lifted it from its base. I stood and turned to the nearest window. The creole guy working the counter pulled off his headphones and sat up.

"Wha'chu tink ya doin', boie?" he asked.

---

[173] American web portal and online service provider based in New York City. It traces its history to an online service known as PlayNET, which went live in November 1985. In the early 90s, AOL grew to become the largest online service, displacing established players like CompuServe and The Source. By 1995, it had over three million users and was the most recognized brand on the web in the United States. AOL provided a dial-up service as well as a web portal, e-mail, instant messaging, and a web browser. In 2001, at the height of its popularity, it purchased the media conglomerate Time Warner in the largest merger in US history. AOL rapidly shrank thereafter, partly due to the decline of dial-up and the rise of broadband. It is still around today, however, thanks to inveterate motherfuckers like me and my pops who won't switch to Gmail.

I saw the whites of his eyes. I grew a sad look.

"I just heard from my girlfriend."

His tamarind face broke into laughter.

"Ya mon. I be knowin' dat one. But don' teak it out on da po' computah."

I raised my brow at a slant. I set the monitor down and took a deep breath. I blew it out cool across the keyboard. I steadied my fingers and looked at the screen. The title of Tanya's next email was "I thought I was done." I opened it wearing the expression of a bomb technician clipping the yellow wire instead of the green. It started, *But I'm not.* Then it devolved into this:

I want your penis. I want your hard body. Arghghghg! I want it up against a counter or a wall . . . yesss . . . a wall. A cold wall to contrast with the warmth of the bodies. And your lips biting and sucking my neck. And you so fucking teased that I keep denying you, and you keep coming on to me relentlessly, and I give in. I need sex, Johann. I need to hear moans and see your face covered in a mask of sexual pleasure. Fuck . . . Oh, and I've prolly read that letter you sent me fifteen times.

It felt like I was reading the diary of a sea creature in heat. I imagined Tanya, legs akimbo, being fucked by a bundle of drooling cocks. I forgot about the other two emails she'd sent. I clicked Reply and typed. My fingers were little cannons firing lead balls for words. I scolded her mercilessly for asking if she could screw Amos or other girls. I told her I was shocked she was having these urges after only ten days, that I couldn't even jerk off without her, and that even her desire to fuck me was worrisome because it seemed like an afterthought. I wrote that I hoped this was a sick joke. I concluded by asking if she even liked my love letter. I sent the email and waited for her response. Twenty minutes later, it came. She began with "Sigh." Then she wrote: *Yes, sweetie, I was kidding about Amos and the other girls.* She said of course she loved my letter, that she'd printed it out, read it and reread it, felt comforted by it, cried because of it. This gave way to her own brand of scolding:

I've written you two other letters that had absolutely nothing to do with sex. Ones where I'm pining for your company, wishing you were here. Where's your reaction to those, damnit?

I remembered the other two emails. I vowed to check them afterwards. I continued reading. She proclaimed that she loved her men, treated them right, massaged them, adored them. She admonished me for having left so quickly, for using an intimidating tone, and for squashing the leap of joy her heart had felt when she'd seen I'd responded. She ended with an outburst akin to mine:

GODDAMNIT, JOHANN. WHY ARE YOU DOING THIS? YOU KNOW I WAS JOKING! That's how I am. God, why? I don't understand.

My stomach puckered. I ran to the bathroom and retched. I came back and checked her first email. The title was "Beautiful. Beautiful. You're beautiful as the sun. Wonderful. Wonderful. You're wonderful as they come." I felt like a pile of leprous scabs. I clicked it and read. She declared that I'd rendered her speechless. She wrote, *I don't think there is any way possible to let you know how much that letter eased my pain.* I crumbled to the floor. I rolled around and eyeballed the ceiling. The creole guy at the front desk ignored me. I wondered why, then I remembered this was Belize.

I picked myself up and finished reading. Tanya had written some very nice things about me. She said I was talented, passionate, and intelligent, that she admired my willingness to learn from my mistakes, and my "eagerness to experience the nearly sickening glory that is inherent in loving and being loved." She also expressed her woes: how guilty she felt for having left Danny, and how unstable she was with our love being so new. She wrote that she feared my anger, that suddenly I'd realize how blind I'd been and see her for the weak and pathetic woman she was. She ended the letter with a PS.

I'm beginning to cry now as I press the Send button. I'll never forget the feeling of peace I get when I feel your chest up against my back. I love you. I miss you. I need you.

My throat was a sandbox. I grabbed my water bottle and chugged. My nerves settled and I opened her second missed email. It was more emotional gushing, then a little summary of the book *Jazz*[174] by Toni Morrison.[175] She ended with a strange but endearing rant.

Why couldn't you tell me how you felt before you left? Why did our last night together have to hurt so much? I love when you pull me towards you, trying to get my body to cling to your body like a puzzle piece. That's what I feel—incomplete.

---

[174] Historical novel by Pulitzer and Nobel Prize-winning American author Toni Morrison. Most of the book's narrative takes place in Harlem during the 1920s; however, as various characters' pasts are explored, the narrative extends back to the mid-19th-century American South. *Jazz* is the second installment of Morrison's Dantesque trilogy on African American history, beginning with *Beloved* (1987) and ending with *Paradise* (1997).

[175] American novelist, essayist, book editor, and college professor (February 18, 1931 – August 5, 2019). Her first novel, *The Bluest Eye*, was published in 1970; however, it was *Song of Solomon* (1977) which brought her national attention and won the National Book Critics Circle Award. In 1988, Morrison won the Pulitzer Prize for *Beloved* (1987). She gained worldwide recognition when she was awarded the Nobel Prize in Literature in 1993. Although her novels typically concentrate on black women, Morrison did not identify her works as feminist. When asked in a 1998 interview, "Why distance oneself from feminism?" she replied: "In order to be as free as I possibly can, in my own imagination, I can't take positions that are closed. Everything I've ever done, in the writing world, has been to expand articulation, rather than to close it, to open doors, sometimes, not even closing the book – leaving the endings open for reinterpretation, revisitation, a little ambiguity." She went on to state that she thought it "off-putting to some readers, who may feel that I'm involved in writing some kind of feminist tract. I don't subscribe to patriarchy, and I don't think it should be substituted with matriarchy. I think it's a question of equitable access, and opening doors to all sorts of things."

I wrote her an email apologizing for my outburst. She wrote one back apologizing for hers. I wrote her another apologizing further. She responded in kind, and we went back and forth, back and forth. By the end of it, I was so drained I could have crawled into a hole and died. I sent a final message and paid the creole dude at the front desk. He took the stack of money and smirked.

"Betta get some sleep, Romeo."

I chuckled and walked back to the room. I stretched out on the bed and flatlined.

I needed to be alone today. I got up, packed some snacks, and hit the road. I forwent a taxi and walked the 1.5 km to Cahal Pech.[176] It was a sight to behold: stone temples with black steps and trees growing on their shoulders like freshly woken ogres. I wandered around the complex deep in thought. My mind was a tilted maze, and my consciousness was a greased BB speeding around its corners. I pondered the nature of my relationship with Tanya. I pulled at its stem and fondled its thorns and lifted its petals. I thought about the guys and our current trip. Here we were amid all this jungle and magic, but I'd spent half the time glued to a computer screen. I spotted a granite throne across the courtyard. I walked to it and sat. Its base was cool and rough. Its back was wide and freckled with lichen. I felt like the ruler of an ancient empire—one that had lost its glory but could still recapture it.

Tourists trickled in. I lost my verve and split. I met

---

[176] Maya site located near the town of San Ignacio. It was a palatial, hilltop home for an elite Maya family, and evidence of continuous habitation has been dated to as far back as 1200 BCE, making it one of the oldest recognizably Maya sites in Western Belize. The name *Cahal Pech* means Place of the Ticks in the Yucatec Maya language. (I hate ticks.)

with the guys for dinner. We sauced[177] at a Chinese joint at the edge of town. The waitress was a nice old lady with a black bun and a knuckle for a chin. She served us sweet and sour chicken, moo shu pork, and shrimp fried rice. We crushed our plates and guzzled beers. We paid the bill and tipped a guap.[178] My homies had it in them to keep partying.

"Lemme check my email first," I said.

They groaned and waved me on. I laughed and went to the internet café. Creole Joe was at the desk, wearing his headphones. He chuckled when he saw me.

"Back fa' roun' two, eh?"

I snorted and got on a computer. I logged onto AOL and checked my email. There was one from Tanya. Its title was "Anything Goes." I couldn't fathom what that meant. I was afraid I'd open it and all the mythical beings ever to terrorize the minds of madwomen would whirl out of the screen and burrow themselves in my ears, eyes, and mouth. I clicked on it with a cringe. It started with lyrics by Cole Porter.[179] They concerned hymns, limbs, and nudist parties in studios. I could imagine Tanya in all of it. She asked me if I thought it was cute. I mumbled to myself, "Not especially." I continued reading. She recounted how the previous evening she'd gone with Gay Amos to a meteor shower.

---

[177] To eat, especially a lot of delicious food.

[178] African-American Vernacular English term for a large sum of money.

[179] American composer and songwriter (June 9, 1891 – October 15, 1964). Many of his songs became standards noted for their witty lyrics, and many of his scores found success on Broadway and in film. Unlike many Broadway composers, Porter wrote the lyrics as well as the music for his songs. "Anything Goes" was one of his more popular songs in the 1930s. It was also the title of the first of his five shows featuring "the undisputed First Lady of the musical comedy stage," Ethel Merman. Porter loved Merman's loud, brassy voice and enormous stage presence. This combination was perfect for said play as its story revolved around madcap antics aboard an ocean liner bound from New York to London.

We sat out there and sang songs like "Build Me Up, Buttercup"[180] *and "Bohemian Rhapsody"*[181] *waaaay off-key. It was riotously fun, but we didn't see any meteors; we prolly scared them away.*

I sympathized with the meteors. I waded through the rest of her email. It was a whole fuck-load about Danny. She couldn't seem to get over the guilt of having broken up with him. She said that a few short months ago she was begging him to come to San Diego, that despite getting no sleep, the poor bastard would get in his car and drive down to calm her worries and warm her bed. She finished with a bit about me.

I beg for you to subdue my heart, to help me swallow the lump that is choking my throat. I think I picked a strange word to describe it—swallow. But it fits. We fit. I love you.

I'm not sure how I responded—prolly with something trite about how she should channel her emotions into positive things. I didn't have much else to give. All I could think about was old Danny.

---

[180] Song written by English songwriters Mike d'Abo and Tony Macaulay. Released by The Foundations in 1968 with Colin Young singing lead vocals. It hit No. 1 on the Cash Box Top 100 and No. 3 on the US Billboard Hot 100 in early 1969. The song was later featured in the 1998 comedy film *There's Something About Mary* and is one of the 7th-inning stretch tunes played at Angel Stadium, home of the Los Angeles Angels.

[181] Song by the British rock band Queen. It was written by lead singer Freddie Mercury for the band's 1975 album *A Night at the Opera*. The song is a six-minute suite, notable for its lack of a refraining chorus. It consists of several sections: an intro, a ballad segment, an operatic passage, a hard rock jag, and a reflective coda. The song is one of the few from the 1970s progressive rock movement to achieve widespread success, topping the UK Singles Chart for nine weeks and becoming the country's third best-selling single of all time. In the United States, the song peaked at number nine in 1976, but reached a new peak of number two on the Billboard Hot 100 after being used in the film *Wayne's World* (1992). *The New York Times* commented that "the song's most distinct feature is the fatalistic lyrics." Mercury refused to explain his composition other than to say it was about relationships. The band protects the song's secret to this day.

I woke up to the sun frying my legs. A little voice whispered, "Get movin'." I kicked out of bed and rinsed off. I rousted the guys and we split. I wanted to do something drastic. I led us through the patchwork of shanties, shacks, and churches and into the bush where the roads were dirt, and the trees were green cathedrals for parrots. We came to a clearing in the foliage. We saw a tributary of the Macal River.[182] Behind it was a tree-studded rock wall. It was easily a hundred feet tall. I eyed it and pointed.

"We're jumpin' off that shit."

I dove into the murky water. I swam across the tributary and onto the rocks. My homies followed *tout suite.* We gathered and scoped the scene. We saw boulders with handholds up to a point. At sixty feet, the rock turned flat and lost its grips. I mapped my route and bared my teeth.

"You really gonna do this?" Tim asked.

"Chea hea."

I steadied myself and grabbed the rock. I shimmied up, up, up like a rhesus macaque. I got to the top and faced the river. I released a roar that made skin curl and bones shiver. I was the biggest, baddest motherfucker on tha block.

"Y'all bitch-ass niggaz can suck this cock!"

I leaped from the stone and into the sky. My body was free although it might die. I flailed my arms like they were on fire. I'd say I was fearless, but I'd be a liar. Then with the greatness of Big Daddy Kane,[183] I pimp-slapped the

---

[182] River running through the jungle-laden Cayo District in Western Belize. Sites along the river include the ancient Mayan town of Cahal Pech and the Belize Botanic Gardens.

[183] Antonio Hardy (born September 10, 1968), better known by his stage name Big Daddy Kane, is an American rapper who began his career in 1986 as a member of the *Juice Crew*—a hip hop collective composed largely of Queensbridge, New York-based artists. His stage name came from a slick variation on "Caine," David Carradine's character from the TV show *Kung Fu,* and a character called "Big Daddy," whom actor Vincent Price played in the film *Beach Party*

liquid and out went my brain.

I came to a half-second later. I swam to the surface and saw my bros. They were cheering and hooting and screaming my name. Maybe not that last part, but it's nice to dream.

We all jumped off the rocks. Tim captured it on film. We cut back through the bush at sundown. We had dinner at our little Chinese joint, then, like a faithful puppy, I went and checked my email. I had one from Tanya. She said she'd gotten hit on twice while working the silver stand. She claimed ignorance as to why. She asked, "Is it wrong to use my looks to get free ice cream?" She rambled about Danny—something to do with him going to visit family in Pennsylvania. She asked when I was coming back. She recalled I'd mentioned the 30th but said she couldn't hang out that day because it was Shoshi's birthday. She ended with a little request:

Look up at the sky tonight. I bet you'll see shooting stars.

I responded with an email of decent length. I held my anger on the ice cream question and recounted the tale of the rock jumps. I ended by telling her I'd fly back on the 31st and drive up to see her that day. *I'll change my ticket tonight*, I wrote.

I paid Creole Joe and went back to the room. The guys were stretched across their beds, fondling their balls and watching TV. I stripped to my skivvies and joined them.

(1963). *Rolling Stone* ranked his song "Ain't No Half-Steppin'" number 25 on its list *The 50 Greatest Hip-Hop Songs of All Time*. Kane is widely regarded as a top rapper during the "golden age" of hip hop (1986–1997); however, his experimentation with R&B beats and his alignment to the Five Percent Nation drew criticism.

We watched a few flicks: Rambo,[184] Gremlins,[185] Freddy.[186] The clock struck midnight. My homies were asleep. I remembered Tanya's request. I went to the balcony and looked at the sky. It was awash in swirls of gray and black. A few stars twinkled in the folds. I imagined her in my arms. The buildings, the sky, the jungle, the clouds, melted away. I could feel her growing inside. She blanketed my pain and covered my wounds. I hugged her as tight as I could. She dissolved in my arms like the morning moon. My anxiety surged and my thoughts churned. I came to the realization I had arrived at earlier on that beach in Cancún: I missed Tanya terribly and needed to be home. I called my mother and had her change my leave date to the twentieth.

We got up and packed our shit. We hailed a cab and booked it to Guatemala. Our sights were on Tikal.[187] The

---

[184] 1982 American action film directed by Ted Kotcheff and co-written by Sylvester Stallone, who also stars as Vietnam War veteran John Rambo. In the film, Rambo must rely on his combat and survival skills when a series of brutal events results in him having to endure a massive manhunt by police and government troops in the untamed wilderness near the small town of Hope, Washington.

[185] 1984 American comedy horror film directed by Joe Dante and executively produced by Steven Spielberg. It stars Zach Galligan and Phoebe Cates, with Howie Mandel providing the voice of Gizmo, the main "mogwai" character. The story follows a young man who receives a strange creature called a "mogwai" as a pet, which then spawns other creatures who transform into small, aggressive monsters called "gremlins" who wreak havoc on a town on Christmas Eve. The film draws on legends of folkloric mischievous creatures of the same name that caused malfunctions in the British Royal Air Force during World War II.

[186] Freddy Krueger, villain from the *A Nightmare on Elm Street* film franchise.

[187] Ruin of one of the largest urban centers of the pre-Columbian Maya civilization. It covered an area greater than 16 square kilometers (6.2 sq mi) that included about 3,000 structures in the Petén Basin in what is now northern Guatemala. Population estimates vary from 10,000 to as high as 90,000 inhabitants. Although monumental architecture at the site dates back as far as the 4th century BC, Tikal reached its apogee during the Classic Period, c. 200 to 900. The city

sky was a bog of silver clouds. We cut down a dirt road and into the Great Plaza.[188] The first thing we saw was Temple I.[189] It rose from the ground like a mutant tortoise—its shell was the seat for a great white throne. We stood at its base and faced its peak. We looked across the plaza, past a crumbling acropolis, a lesser temple, and a swath of lime-green grass. We saw Temple III.[190] The fucker was a full building taller. Its belly was hidden by jungle. Its head towered above the canopy like the hood of a druid priest. We walked to it and snapped photos. A spider monkey leaped through the branches overhead. We followed it into the jungle. We lost it near a reed hut. The wind whipped and the sky rumbled. We felt the first drops of rain. We took cover in the hut. We heard a million leaves rustle and hiss, then . . . boom! A bolt of lightning cracked

---

was possibly conquered by Teotihuacán in the 4th century AD. Following the end of the Late Classic Period, no new major monuments were built, and evidence exists that elite palaces were burned. These events were coupled with a gradual population decline, culminating in the site's abandonment by the end of the 10th century. Knowledge of the site was never completely lost in the region, however. Local people knew of its existence and guided expeditions to the ruins, the first of which was in 1848. Thereafter, archeologists came and started to clear, map, and record the ruins. From 1956 through 1970, major archeological excavations and structural restorations were carried out by the University of Pennsylvania's Tikal Project. In 1979, the Guatemalan government began a further archeological project, which continued through to 1984, and brought Tikal to roughly its present state.

[188] Central square and beating heart of Tikal.

[189] Designation given to one of Tikal's major structures, which peaks at 47 meters (154 ft) and is located on the eastern side of the Great Plaza. It is also known as the Temple of the Great Jaguar because of a lintel that represents a king sitting upon a jaguar throne. The structure itself is a funerary temple associated with Jasaw Chan K'awiil I, who ruled Tikal from AD 682–734; his tomb has been located deep within. The temple rises in nine stepped levels, which may be symbolic of the nine levels of the Maya underworld.

[190] Principal temple pyramid at Tikal, standing approximately 55 meters (180 ft) tall. Its summit shrine differs in that it only possesses two rooms instead of the usual three. The temple has been dated to 810 AD using hieroglyphic text. It is associated with the little-known king Dark Sun; it is likely to be his funerary temple.

across the clouds. It was one tremendous glowing root, then split into two, then four, then eight, then twelve. It looked like the family tree of Norse gods. It held its crackling electric grip for a second, then vanished. We shouted in awe. We pulled the ponchos from our packs and slipped them on. Mason checked the map and spotted Temple IV;[191] it was a short walk away. We decided to brave the storm and climb the beast. It was the tallest of the structures at 230 motherfucking feet.

We arrived at the base, dripping with rain. We looked at the stone staircase, which ran through the canopy and into outer space. We put our hands and feet on the steps and worked. We moved at a slow pace, whoofing and panting and sweating. After what felt like an hour, we arrived at the top. The rain stopped, and the winds calmed. A ray of sunlight pierced the cloud cover and gilded the edges of the temples. The trees below became a sea of brightening greens. The people in the plaza were colored ants. The horizon was a pyroclastic flow of yellows and pinks and reds. We stood together and soaked it in. We were buddies, but we felt like kin.

That night we blew it up proper in Flores.[192] We got two double rooms at a swanky hotel, dressed in our only collared shirts, and went to dinner at the nicest joint in town. We ordered a feast fit for *Acan*[193]—baked armadillo,

---

[191] Tallest temple-pyramid at Tikal, measuring 70 meters (230 ft) top to bottom. It marks the reign of Yik'in Chan Kawil, the son of Jasaw Chan K'awiil I, for whom Temple I was built. Temple IV is the largest pyramid built in the Maya region in the 8th century, and as it currently stands is the tallest pre-Columbian structure in the Americas.

[192] Capital of Petén, Guatemala's landlocked, northernmost department. With a population of 13,700 (2003), the old part of the city is located on an island on Lake Petén Itzá connected to the mainland by a short causeway. It is the jumping off point for people interested in visiting Tikal.

[193] Mayan god of wine and intoxication. He has been compared to the Roman god, Bacchus, and the Greek god, Dionysus. His name translates to burp or groan in ancient Mayan, and he is identified with the local brew *balché*—a fermented mixture that contained honey and

grilled venison, turkey tamales, fried plantains, and black bean soup. We washed it down with chocolaty *Moza*[194] beers. We ended the meal with *borrachos*[195] and three shots of Ron Zacapa 23.[196]

We left the restaurant like wild hobos. We kicked in the door of the nearest bar and got more beers, more shots, more fuel. The night took on a grandness I had never seen. There we were, four shitkickers from the hills of Livermore, burning the oil of the gods under the great stone temples of *Yax Mutal*.[197] I ordered a round of *Botran*,[198] and we cheers'd. The rum went down our throats like water fresh from a spring. I excused myself and hit the shitter. I had a long, satisfying piss and ripped a fart that steamed my jeans. I washed my hands and went back out. My homies were talking to a group of girls. I ordered a beer and sat by myself. My mood dipped. I

---

bark of the balché tree. During official ceremonies, ancient Maya consumed balché along with peyote, magic mushrooms, morning glory seeds, and tobacco in hopes of communicating with the gods to obtain divine explanations for things like illness, poor harvests, battle losses, and unfavorable weather.

[194] German-style Bock (strong lager) brewed by Cervecería Centro Americana, based in Guatemala City. It is one of the most popular beers in Guatemala.

[195] Guatemalan dessert cake drenched in rum and sugar syrup. Its name means drunk in Spanish.

[196] Premium, long-aged rum produced in Guatemala by Rum Creation and Products. Created in 1976 to celebrate the one hundredth anniversary of the foundation of Zacapa, a town in eastern Guatemala. Ron Zacapa Centenario 23 used to be known as Ron Zacapa Centenario 23 Años. Its name was changed, as people thought it was a 23-year-old rum instead of a blend of rums between 6 and 23 years old.

[197] Tikal may be derived from "ti ak'al" in the Yucatec Maya language, meaning "at the waterhole"—a possible reference to one of the site's ancient reservoirs. Hieroglyphic inscriptions refer to the ancient city as Yax Mutal, meaning First Mutal. The city may have been called this because the rulers wanted to distinguish themselves as the first city to bear the name. The kingdom was called Mutal. Its precise meaning remains obscure.

[198] Line of rums from Guatemala distilled by the *Industrias Licoreras de Guatemala*, the same distillery that produces the Zacapa line of rums. It is named after the Botran family, who were the first family to produce rum in Guatemala.

thought of my history with this mistress called Travel: my semester in Madrid in the fall of '03, my journey across South America with Mason that summer, my voyage around Turkey, Scandinavia, and the Baltic States in '02, my romp through Asia with my father in '01, my graduation trip through Morocco and half of Europe in 2000, and all those little trips across country I'd taken with my folks as far back as '83. Tears formed around my eyes. I drank my beer and split. I walked down the empty street in a daze. I stopped at the internet place before it closed and sent Tanya a brief email. I went to the room and pulled off my clothes. Sleep washed over me like a cold ocean wave.

We cut to San Ignacio the next morning. We got our old room at our old place and hunkered in for three days. We sauced Chinese food at our favorite spot. We went cliff jumping, bought souvenirs, and watched tons of movies. I spent an inordinate amount of time at the internet café. I wrote Tanya about our adventures in Tikal and our crazy nights, but I made sure to include how much I missed her. I refrained from mentioning my return on the 20th—I wanted it to be a surprise.

For every email I sent, Tanya responded with two. She wrote more stories of guys hitting on her, more rants about her family's financial problems, more tearful passages about the pain she felt for Danny, and paragraph upon paragraph about her incredible shrinking great-granny. She lambasted her mother for running off to El Salvador in the middle of everything. She praised her daddy for making the best of an awful situation and for brightening her days with lemonade and homemade pizza. She professed a keen interest in knowing how many girls had hit on me. I told her about Chrissy Brown Eyes and a few others. She responded, *God, the thought of so many hot girls hitting on you fucking kills me!* I guess I was supposed to feel flattered, but I felt weird. I told her Mason was planning to fuck the hottest of them—Chrissy Brown Eyes—before he left the country. On our last day in San Ignacio, homeboy split to Belize City to do just that.

Tim, Bert, and I went to Belmopan.[199] We caught the one o'clock Mennonite musk bus and arrived at 2:15 p.m. We grabbed our packs from the upper cubbies and got off. Mason was waiting for us outside. His face was plump with blood. His ginger beard looked like a clump of manzanita shavings on fire. He gave us daps and smiled.

"You hit that shit?" I asked.

"Chea hea."

He showed us a few shots of Chrissy posing in her thong. They reminded me of Tanya. I forced her out of my head. We got a room at a cheap motel and hit the Blue Hole.[200] We swam in its icy waters and jumped off the surrounding rocks. We hiked the Hummingbird Loop through the jungle and explored a nearby cave.

By the end of the day, I was covered in mosquito bites. I spread ointment over my body, bought a phone card, and called Tanya. She was surprised to hear from me. Something in her voice sounded strange. I figured she

---

[199] Capital city of Belize with a population of 16,451 (2010). It is the smallest capital city in the continental Americas by population and the third-largest settlement in Belize, behind Belize City and San Ignacio. Belmopan was founded in 1970, 82 kilometers (51 mi) inland, after Hurricane Hattie (1961) destroyed approximately 75% of the houses and businesses in low-lying, coastal Belize City. The new settlement was on better terrain, entailed no costly reclamation of land, and provided an area for industrial growth.

[200] St. Herman's Blue Hole National Park is located just off the Hummingbird Highway in the Cayo District of Belize, near Belmopan. It is over 500 acres (2 km²) in area and contains two cave systems (St. Herman's and Crystal), various natural trails (including the Hummingbird Loop), and the deep, blue jungle pool from which the park gets its name. Not to be confused with the offshore Great Blue Hole, also in Belize.

missed me. I wanted to tell her I was coming home early, but again, I refrained.

We said, "I love you" and hung up. I went back to the room and crashed. I spent the following afternoon chilling with the guys and drinking beers. It was our last day together, but all I could think about was Tanya. I convinced myself that surprising her would be the highlight of my year. I couldn't wait to see the shock on her face when I walked through her front door.

The next morning, I got up early and packed. Bert did, too, as he'd be leaving on the same flight. I told him I'd be back in an hour and to watch my crap. I went to the internet café and checked my email. I already had three from Tanya. The first was a lot about how she hoped she'd get her period in two days. The second was her hating on my "elusive, irritating, and oddly comforting" screenname "Tzerreaw." And the third was her lamenting over being what she described as officially empty.

I have been trying to keep busy so that the temptation to mutilate myself doesn't arise. I miss you terribly. And I miss being able to fill the hole in my heart with your presence.

I didn't know what to make of it. I responded with a sizable email. I told her I missed her like hell. I recounted a few new adventures and said I was sure she'd get her period. I wrote that I hoped my words would fill her up a little. I sat back and pressed Send. I had half an hour to spare. I waited for her response. Thoughts of her being pregnant swarmed my head. They clotted my blood and choked my nerves and rattled my spine. The seconds ticked by like centuries. I was one tick away from losing my shit, then I heard, "You've Got Mail."

I grabbed the mouse and clicked my inbox. I opened the email and read it. Tanya professed her love for public libraries. Then she shifted tracks. *I'm not pregnant,* she wrote. *I took a test a while ago, but I forgot to tell you.* I breathed a sigh of relief. I composed myself and continued reading. She went on to tell the story of some fat, greasy Middle Eastern guy who'd hit on her from his car window while she'd been night-jogging. She said he'd offered to give her a ride home, and when she'd refused, he'd followed alongside her making kissy noises and staring at her. She said she'd contemplated banging on the door of the nearest house. *Eventually he gave up, though,* she wrote.

I wanted to send her an email expressing my concern, but I didn't have time. I logged off the computer, paid for my session, and rushed back to the room. I said late to Tim and Mason and wished them luck on their journey. I asked them how far down the map they'd go. They both grinned.

"As far as we need to," Mason said.

My face tightened with jealousy. I played it off with a lighthearted chuckle. I grabbed my bag and Bert grabbed his. We took a cab to Goldson Airport and checked in. We had a half hour before boarding. We went to a bar and got Belikins. We picked a table and sat. Bert ran a hand through his curls and fixed his Hawaiian shirt. He popped the top off his beer and took a sip.

"You ready for this shit?" he asked.

I cracked my beer and guzzled it.

"I sure as fuck hope so," I said.

PART THREE

We landed in San Diego in the afternoon. We got our bags and said late. Bert bounced to meet a friend in the center. I took a cab to Tim's, got my car, and drove to Reseda. I thought about Tanya the whole way. I planned what I'd do, how I'd act, what I'd say. I arrived in the early evening. The sky was a levitating stew of pink and blue and gray. I parked my car in front of the Gladstone's rotting lawn. I got out and went up the walkway. My heart pumped like a piston. My forehead dripped with sweat and my ears burned. I stepped onto the porch and noticed that only the screen door was closed. I could see through the kitchen and into the backyard. I fixed my collar and brushed my shirt. I wiped the sweat from my brow and cracked my neck. I pointed a finger and moved it toward the doorbell. As I touched it, I saw Tanya. She walked from the hall without noticing me. She wore blue bellbottoms with patched knees and a white top. Her hair was over her shoulders. She was barefoot and braless. She held a cordless phone to her ear and laughed with her teeth out. I waited for her to notice me. She said something in Spanish about how her summer was going. She turned and faced me. Her look went from mild enjoyment to surprise. She told the person on the other line that her friend had arrived. She opened the screen door with the phone still to her ear. She grinned and raised a finger and talked for thirty seconds more. She hung up and fluffed out her hair. Then she hugged me.

"Oh my God, you're here so early," she said.

She put her head under my nose. Her hair smelled of lilies. I squeezed her and gave her a kiss. She kissed back and pulled away.

"What happened to coming on the thirty-first?"

"I decided to come early and surprise you. That's good, right?"

"No, of course, of course. I just wasn't expecting you, darling. But look at you—you're all tan and ripped and skinny. You look like Danny did when we'd spend days on the beach together."

"Can we please not talk about him for at least the first hour?"

"Oh c'mon. I'm saying you look hot. Mia and Alejandra went to pick up dinner with my daddy. Let's take your stuff into the guestroom and . . . unpack."

My flaccid penis twitched to life. He grew to a knifepoint behind my boxers. I followed Tanya into the guestroom and dropped my pack. She closed the door and swayed up to me. I heard the lust rattle in her guts. She slid her hand around my groin and kissed me. The doorknob twisted and the door creaked open. I looked through the crack. I saw a wired eyeball floating in the dark. A pinched mouth formed underneath.

"*Mantén la puerta abierta,*" it spat. Keep the door open.

Triple-G pushed the door half-open. She stood at the threshold and stared me down. Her hair had turned a shade whiter. She'd shrunk two inches and grown a longer nose. I simpered and nodded. Tanya inhaled and turned around.

"*Sí, madre. Lo siento,*" she said. Yes, Gramma. I'm sorry.

Triple-G scowled and shuffled off. Tanya looked at me and smiled.

"I think we need to go get ice cream for dessert."

I smiled back. Tanya put on her socks and shoes and grabbed her bag. She told her granny we were headed to the grocery store. She kissed the grumbling old coot and bounced out the screen door. I followed her and chuckled. We got in my car and drove around the neighborhood. It was nighttime now. Illuminated streetlights were on most corners. We spotted a willow tree in plenty of darkness. We parked in its umbra and unbuckled our seatbelts. We went at each other like mad badgers. We crashed over our seats and spilled into the back. We pulled off our shoes and socks and tore off our clothes. Tanya straddled my waist and slid my cock into her vagina. It felt like the inside of a hot calzone. I gripped her bony hips and thrust at an angle. She put her hands on the ceiling and screamed. I felt her labia convulse around my shaft. She mouthed, "I'm coming."

"I am, too," I cried.

I thought of pulling out and shooting on my stomach. I remembered the disaster of our last night together. I buried my cock to the hilt. My cum raced upward and exploded in her cervix. The guilty weakness of love seized my heart. I fell back and crossed my arms. Tanya made her lips into an O and expelled a column of air. She fished a wad of tissues from her bag and wiped her vagina. She slid into the front seat and stared at the foggy windshield. I crawled into the driver's seat and touched her hand.

"What's wrong?" I asked.

She looked at her toes and sniffled.

"I'm realizing something."

"What's that?"

"That you really did damage my love for you the last night we were together."

"But I thought we worked through that while I was gone?"

"Johann, listen to what you're saying. How could we have possibly worked through anything while you were gone?"

"Then what was all that about you needing me to come back to fill your empty heart?"

"I did want that. But now that you're here and we've made love, I've realized the depth of the damage you inflicted. And I can't ignore it anymore."

I felt like the lowest slick of web-footed slop to ever drag its sorry ass out of a swamp. My jaw twizzled in its cradle and my eyes barfed tears. I grabbed the wad of tissue Tanya had used on her pussy and blew my nose in it. I slumped over in my seat.

"Is there anything I can do to make it up to you?" I groaned.

"I don't know."

I grabbed my pants and reached into the front right pocket. I pulled out a small box and handed it to her. She opened it and smiled.

"I bought it for you in San Ignacio. It's sterling silver and amber."

She lifted the necklace and clasped it around her neck. The teardrop of amber shone beautifully in the low light. She flattened her hand and held it over the pendent. She looked at me and raised the corner of her mouth.

"This is a start."

"Okay," I sighed.

I spent the month before fall semester trying to repair our relationship. I drove to Reseda every weekend and took Tanya to her favorite spots. We went to LACMA,[201] Venice Beach, Inspiration Point,[202] The Getty Museum,[203] and the

---

[201] Los Angeles County Museum of Art (LACMA) – Located on Wilshire Boulevard in the Miracle Mile area of Los Angeles. It was founded in 1961 and is the largest art museum in the western United States, holding more than 150,000 works of various types including modern, contemporary, American, Latin American, Asian, Greek, Roman, Etruscan, and others.

[202] Vista point located in Will Rogers State Historic Park, the former estate of American humorist Will Rogers. The park lies in the Santa Monica Mountains in Los Angeles, California.

[203] Art museum in Los Angeles housed on two campuses: the Getty Center and Getty Villa. The Getty Center is located in the Brentwood neighborhood and features pre-20th-century European paintings, drawings, illuminated manuscripts, sculptures, decorative arts, and early to modern photographs. The original Getty Museum, the Getty Villa, is located in the Pacific Palisades neighborhood and displays art from Ancient Greece, Rome, and Etruria—a region in central Italy that

Rose Bowl Flea Market.[204] I bought her gifts of silk and gemstones and treated her to nice meals. I did my damnedest to get in good with her besties. I met the silver stand crew and spent a precious minute with Zulma, Amos, and Shoshi.

Meanwhile, I scrambled to get my life set up in San Diego. Bert had another year at SDSU,[205] and Mason had just gotten into UCSD, so we'd agreed on the trip to rent a place together. Since Bert was now in Livermore with his folks and Mason was still on the road with Tim, the responsibility of finding an apartment fell on me. I spent weeks looking at places, using Tim's empty flat as my base. I settled on a three-bedroom in Chula Vista.[206] I took the biggest of the bedrooms—which happened to have a private bath—because, hey. I prepared for my coming responsibilities as the *Guardian* Features Editor. I built a schedule and planned meetings and cleaned my tiny office. I enrolled in my classes and bought tons of school supplies. It was a wild balancing act, but I managed to keep everything from crashing to the ground.

School started on September 20th. I was swamped with classes and work for the newspaper. Tanya begged me to join the dance team with her. Despite my fear and lack of skill, I agreed. She reciprocated by attending my *Guardian*

---

was home to the Etruscans. (I once saw actor Christopher Lloyd at The Getty. But that's a story for another book.)

[204] Large swap meet held on the grounds of the Rose Bowl stadium in Pasadena, a city in Los Angeles County. The swap meet has thousands of dealers displaying old world antiques, California pottery, vintage clothing, and other items. It has been held every second Sunday of the month since 1967.

[205] San Diego State University (SDSU) is a public research university in San Diego, California. Founded in 1897 as San Diego Normal School, it is the third-oldest university in the 23-member California State University (CSU) system.

[206] Second-largest city in the San Diego metropolitan area, with a population of 243,916 (2010). Chula Vista is Spanish for Beautiful View. The city is so named because of its scenic location between the San Diego Bay and coastal mountain foothills.

meetings. She made staff writer within two weeks and started her sex advice column called The Pleasure Trove. She brought loads of her crap over and spent the night frequently; I didn't blame her, as she shared a small flat with three Korean girls who hated her guts. I hoped this would bring us closer together. It seemed to at first, but as the weeks passed, I could feel our connection fading. I knew it wasn't just about what had happened that cursed night. Since the age of thirteen, Tanya had never really been alone. Before me, it was Danny. Before him, it was a guy named Mateo, and before him, it was some other guy. With her history of dating and her enormous family and friend base, Tanya didn't know the meaning of alone. I, on the other hand, was more than familiar with it; I'd only had one other girlfriend, and when I wasn't mingling with buds or kin, I was savoring my solitude and attempting to write.

On the night of October 20th, we had dance practice. We did the tango, foxtrot, quickstep, samba, rhumba, cha-cha, jive, and waltz. I paired with Tanya for a couple songs. She never faced me and hardly smiled. I felt like I was dancing with a plastic doll. I hid my disappointment as best I could.

Practice ended late. We walked to Tanya's as she lived near campus. Her flatmates were in the kitchen watching TV and eating kimchi. They sneered at us and returned to their business. We went to Tanya's matchbox of a room and closed the door. We sat on her single bed and pulled off our shoes. Our feet were bruised and swollen. Our calves ached and our spines burned. I put my hands on Tanya's shoulders and dug in my thumbs. She usually turned into goo, but this time she remained stiff. I pulled my hands away and stared at her back.

"What's going on?" I asked.

I heard sniffling. She reached up and hooked her hair around her ear. She turned and poked her teeth over her shoulder. I said it before she could.

"Do we need a break?"

The second the words left my mouth, I wanted to snatch them from the air. She faced me and smiled.

"Would you be okay with that?"

"I don't know if okay is the right word. But this isn't working, and I don't know what else to do."

She put her hands on my knees and studied my eyes.

"You seem so subdued."

"I'm not subdued. Just resigned. I know you've never really had a chance to be alone, and I want to give you that. Plus, I'm too tired to fight."

She buried her face in my chest and wept. I put my chin on her head and cried silently. We held each other for a few moments. Then she looked up at me.

"Thank you for this."

"No problem."

The next few days were torture. I spent every private moment fretting, screaming, and crying. I refused to sleep in my bed. I coaxed Bert and Mason into watching movies with me in the living room, then I fell asleep on the couch. I found it hard to even enter my bedroom. Every time I did, I saw a reminder of Tanya—her sandals in my closet, her bellbottoms in my hamper, her dinosaur toothbrush with bitemarks lying on my sink. I spoke to her on the phone two or three times a day. I tried to be cheerful and not let my pain gush into the receiver. Work helped occupy my mind. I studied and had meetings and edited articles.

I went to the *Guardian* that Saturday. I said hello to my coworkers and assembled my section for next week's edition. Halfway through, I stepped outside for some fresh air. I saw Tanya walking toward me. She wore a white hoodie and baggy jeans. Her hair was in a tight ponytail. I forced a smile and said, "Hey." She stopped and handed me a box of orange juice.

"Thought you might be thirsty."

"Thanks. What's up?"

"Nothing. I just wanted to see you. Can we talk?"

"Sure."

I walked with her to a nearby park. We sat on a grassy knoll and faced each other. The sky was a patchwork of clouds. A thread of sunlight poked through and landed on our laps. We enjoyed it in silence for a moment. I spoke first.

"So, what's going on?"

"First of all," she said, pulling a journal from her kangaroo pocket, "I wanted to give you this."

"Jesus, thank you."

She handed me the journal. The cover was embossed with a painting of a bonsai tree. I flipped through the pages and saw she had written me a letter. She covered it with her hand.

"You can read that when I'm gone," she said, blushing.

"Okay. Is that everything?"

"Well, no. I also wanted to say that—"

Her face skewed and her eyes filled with tears.

"Oh Johann. I'm terrified that in all this separation, I'm going to lose you as a friend."

I felt a tinge of disappointment. I steeled my face and put my hand on her knee.

"No matter what the outcome of our separation is, you'll never hafta worry about me not being your friend."

Tears spilled down her cheeks. She leaned forward and tried to kiss me. I held my head back with great restraint. She pounded her thighs with her fists.

"I'm so fucking sorry. I can't control myself these days."

"It's okay."

We parted with a sad hug. She left still crying. I ran to the top of the student center to watch her go. She was out of sight when I got there. I opened the journal to the page with the letter. It was dated the previous day.

Darling Johann,

I can't even begin to describe the gratitude I feel towards you for letting me have this chance to be alone. It isn't so much that you helped me break up with you (I probably would have done it eventually), but you did it with such a good heart and monstrous good intentions. I realize this isn't going to be easy for you. So to show my gratitude and support, I give you this journal as a vent for your complex emotions during this trying time. I hope you like it. The cover reminded me of some of the wonderful paintings we saw together at LACMA.

Good love and luck, darling.

I love you,

Tanya

P.S. I miss you.

P.P.S. A lot.

Over the next ten days, we only saw each other at dance practice. We communicated via email and agreed that if either of us dated or slept with someone, we'd be honest about it and remain friends. We exchanged compliments and encouraged one another to do good things. We avoided labels but acknowledged that if we ever did get back together, this period of personal space and reflection would create a strong foundation.

We had practice the Monday after Halloween. We went over some moves, then got in a group for a pep talk from our instructor. Tanya sat next to me. She was wearing a purple sarong and a black tank top. Her butterscotch hair was in a half ponytail. Her arms and legs were bronzed and shaved. I tried to keep my distance. She scooted into my crotch and pulled my arms around her neck. I smelled her vanilla perfume. It obliterated my will to resist.

The pep talk ended at 11:15 p.m. Tanya invited me over to "catch up." I agreed reluctantly. We walked to her place, entered her room, and closed the door. We sat on her bed and looked at each other. She put her hand on my knee.

"What are we doing?" I asked.

Her expression softened.

"I know we agreed we weren't gonna use labels," she said. "But do you know what we've been these past ten days?"

"What?"

"We've been *lovers*."

"I'm not sure what you mean by that."

"I mean, lovers like the olden days—admirers from afar."

"Okay?"

"Anyways, this time apart has made me realize that I don't wanna be apart anymore."

"Really?"

"Yes."

"What are you saying then?"

She reached up and clicked off the lights. We fucked until the clock dropped.

Tanya and I were a couple again. Things seemed to improve. We danced at practice and studied together. We shopped and cooked and took weekend trips. She spent most nights at my place. We screwed like two crackheads in a trunk. It drove Mason and Bert nuts. She appeased them by giving them shoulder massages and making pupusas. I wasn't too thrilled with the former; the latter mostly made up for it.

December 14th was my birthday. Tanya gave me an Albanian dictionary and sucked me dry. Afterward, she told me of her plans to go to El Salvador for Christmas. I was bummed, but I understood. I wanted to get something nice for her return. I knew she liked old books by female authors. I spent a week searching online. I found a gorgeous first edition of *Sons*[207] by Pearl S. Buck.[208] I dropped a pretty penny and had it shipped. It arrived the day after she left. I packed it with my crap and split to Livermore. I spent Christmas with my folks and drank and ate. I chatted with Tanya a few times on the phone. She sounded annoyed with her mother but happy to see the rest of her family. She told me she'd be back in LA on the 30th. We made plans to see each other in the new year. I told her I had a little present for her. She giggled and said she had one for me too.

My folks and I went to a New Year's Eve party at my aunt's in Moraga.[209] She had it catered by a fancy Mexican seafood joint and bought every kind of booze. I stuffed my face with crab enchiladas and shrimp tacos. I pounded a

---

[207] 1932 historical fiction novel by American author Pearl S. Buck. It is the second book in *The House of Earth* trilogy, preceded by *The Good Earth* and followed by *A House Divided*.

[208] Pearl Sydenstricker Buck (June 26, 1892 – March 6, 1973), also known by her Chinese name Sai Zhenzhu, was an American writer, novelist, and daughter of missionaries to China who spent most of her life before 1934 in Zhenjiang, a city on the southern bank of the Yangtze River. She wrote extensively about her time in China. Her second novel *The Good Earth,* a dramatization of family life in a Chinese village in the early 20th century, was the bestselling novel in the United States in both 1931 and 1932 and won the Pulitzer Prize for Fiction in 1932. In 1938, Buck won the Nobel Prize in Literature; she was the first American woman to do so. In her speech to the Academy, she stated, "I am an American by birth and by ancestry," but "my earliest knowledge of story, of how to tell and write stories, came to me in China."

[209] Town in Contra Costa County, California, in the San Francisco Bay Area. As of 2010, it had a population of 16,016 people. The town is named in honor of Joaquín Moraga, member of the famed "Californio" (native Californian Hispanic) family, and grandson of José Joaquín Moraga, a famous 18th century expeditionary of *Alta California*—a former territory of Mexico which included the modern US states of California, Nevada, and Utah, and parts of Arizona, Wyoming, Colorado, and New Mexico.

six-pack of Negra Modelo[210] and shot after shot of *Patrón Añejo*.[211] The clock struck midnight. The champagne popped and everyone cheered. I wished I had a pair of lips to kiss. My phone buzzed in my pocket. I pulled it out and checked the face. I saw it was Tanya calling. I smiled and stumbled outside. I went in my parents' car to avoid the noise. I answered the call and said, "Happy New Year, baby." I heard sniffles in reply.

"What's wrong?' I asked.

I heard drunken cheers and a door slam. Then it was quiet.

"Johann, *please* hear me out," Tanya said.

"Okay?"

"I'm at a party right now at Shoshi's. I came thinking it was just gonna be our little group and a few others, but it turns out that one of Shoshi's friends, whom I'm not really friends with, knows Danny and invited him without telling Shoshi. Anyways, I was drunk by the time he got here. And he was drunk too, and when we saw each other, we knew we had to talk, so we went in Shoshi's room and started talking, and this led to crying, and I massaged Danny's back to make him feel better, and one thing led to another—"

She sobbed. "And . . . and—"

"And what?" I screamed.

"Oh Johann, we fucking made out."

It stung but not terribly. I reeled in my anger.

"Are you sure that's all?"

"Yes. Anyways, you can't be too mad at me. You know how slaphappy I get when I drink."

---

[210] Lager first brewed in Mexico by Austrian immigrants. Its full name is *Cerveza Negra Modelo*. There is often confusion about the gender agreement in the name; however, Negra, which in Spanish means black or dark, modifies Cerveza, meaning beer, not Modelo, which means model or example.

[211] Blend of Patrón Silver tequila aged in French, Hungarian, and American oak for at least one year.

"Is that really your fucking excuse?"

"No. But it's true. And speaking of the truth, I hafta come clean about something else."

"Jesus Christ, what?"

"Promise you won't get mad?"

"Absolutely not."

"Well, I'm telling you anyway. After the thing happened with Danny, everybody kept getting more drunk, and I lost control of myself and, well, on a dare from lord knows who, I straddled Amos and gave him a hickey on his neck."

"You gotta be fucking kidding me."

"I'm not, Johann. I hope you can forgive me."

She sobbed again. I said goodbye and hung up. I looked out the window at the party raging in my aunt's living room.

Some fuckin' new year, I thought.

School started that Monday. I met with Tanya after class. She apologized for her behavior. I wanted to stay angry, but I didn't have the strength. I apologized for exploding. I gave her the book I'd ordered, and she gave me a wooden mask from El Salvador, and we fucked to make up. Things clunked along for the next month. We tried to get back into our old groove but it wasn't the same. Our sex life flagged. Tanya tried to spice it up by having us explore each other's bodies. In her mind, this meant avoiding the connect-the-dots line from mouth to ears to neck to nipples to nuts. Instead, she wanted us to concentrate on the body's "hidden erogenous zones" like the back, shoulders, butt cheeks, ribcage, hipbones, underarms, and taint. It was interesting for a bit. But I soon grew tired of having my armpits smooched when all I wanted was my cock sucked. This frustrated Tanya. She vowed to make a "real lover" out of me yet.

The Saturday before Valentine's Day, we were invited to a Hugs and Kisses party. Tanya wore her knee-high stiletto boots, a sea-green tube top, and a black skirt that barely covered her ass. I wore a collared shirt and some Axe. She begged me to wear skinny jeans, but I couldn't be asked. We showed up at the party at eight. Her friend Kaleb, who'd invited us, answered the door. He was a portly, balding man with a silver beard and a handlebar mustache. I wondered how the hell he knew Tanya. He let us in with a precious smile. He eyed Tanya and lifted her hand.

"You look stunning," he said, spinning her in a slow circle.

She blushed and puckered her strawberry lips.

"Thanks, darlin'."

They hugged and kissed each other's cheeks. Kaleb turned and looked at me. His face stiffened.

"And this must be Johann."

"You got it," I said.

"Lovely to finally meet you."

"Likewise."

He led us around the room. Every time he introduced another of his fabulous friends, he encouraged us to give them hugs and kisses. I wished I'd brought my Belizean machete. I'd have loved to have seen the look on those cocksuckers' faces when I pulled my steel bitch from her sheath. I feigned politeness as best I could. When the shitshow ended, I availed myself of the punch bowl. I got wicked, steaming drunk. Tanya got tipsy herself and the night slipped away. By 2:00 a.m., people were outro. Tanya and I were too ripped to drive. Kaleb offered us his guestroom.

"It has a queen-sized bed and a half bath. I'll make breakfast in the morning."

I was in a spot to think him nice. I said thank you and he eyed me dryly.

"Anything for Tanya."

He ushered us into the room and closed the door.

Tanya plopped on the bed and pulled off her boots. She spread her legs and fingered her pussy over her white lace thong.

"Know what I want you to do?"

"What's that?" I said, undoing my belt.

"First, I want you to take off your pants. "

"Okay."

"Then I want you to spit on your hand."

"Uh-huh."

"Then lean back—"

"Yeah."

"And slap me in the fucking face."

"Huh?"

"You heard me. I want you to spit on your hand and slap me in the face."

"Why?"

"Because it's primal. And it gets my pussy wet."

I opened my hand and looked at it. My palm flattened and my fingers sharpened. The muscles around my back tightened. My spine lit up like a lightsaber. I mouthed a wad and spat it in my hand. I drew back my arm and swung. My palm struck Tanya's cheek; it sounded like a gunshot. Her head bobbled in its socket. She fell back on her elbows and coughed. I felt guilty. She put her hand to the blossoming mar on her face and smiled.

"That was awesome," she said, breathing heavily.

My cock got hard. I tore off my pants and shirt. I leaned in to mount her. She wound back and slapped me. The force made my eyes rattle. The sting spread into my jawbone. I cringed with pain. The pain became anger. I clenched my teeth and spiked my eyebrows. The grayness of death filled my psyche. I cocked my arm and released it. My palm hit Tanya's face like a bomb blast. She flew off the bed and collapsed on the floor. Her bones clattered on the hardwood. The sound shook me from my trance. I felt sick to my stomach. I reached down to help her. She looked up at me with the eyes of a crazed witch. She stood, walked around, and pushed me on the bed. My cock was still hard. She got on top and slipped it in. Her vagina was sopping wet. I opened my mouth to moan. My soul dropped on a speeding elevator to hell.

Our sex life advanced. We did every dirty thing imaginable, plus a few more. Tanya always tested my boundaries. Sometimes I liked it, sometimes not. One time she really pissed me off. I had just finished feeding her my cum from a shot glass and was basking in my nasty pride when out of nowhere she said, "Would you ever let me fuck you in the ass with a strap-on?"

I nearly retched on the carpet. I looked her in the eyes and said no. She slumped her shoulders and frowned.

"But why not? Shoshi's boyfriend lets her do it to him."

"I don't give a fuck what Shoshi's boyfriend lets her do to him. There's no way on God's green earth I'm gonna let you ream my asshole with a plastic dick."

"Jeez, fine . . . then would you ever go down on a guy in front of me?"

"Fuck no."

"Would you let a guy go down on you?"

"Absolutely not."

"Would you at least make out with a guy?"

"No."

She crossed her arms and pouted.

"You're boring."

"I'm not boring. I'm just not into guys."

"What about other girls? You'd be down for that, wouldn't you?"

"Normally, yes. But this is a monogamous relationship, Tanya. I'm not trying to include other people."

"Yeah, we'll see. Anyways, the very least you could do for me is some penis exercises. You're constantly missing my G-spot when we fuck, and I hafta finger myself to make up for it."

"Penis exercises?"

"Yeah. Like that stuff on the internet where the guy stretches his penis so it gets bigger."

"Are you saying I have a small dick?"

"No, silly, your dick is fine. It's just that Danny's dick was slightly bigger, and I got used to it."

My manhood deflated like a punctured colostomy bag. I slumped into a pile of flesh. Tanya grabbed my shoulder and squeezed it with her fingertips.

"Oh, quit being so dramatic. If it's any consolation, your cum tastes better than his."

I leered at her. I went to sleep without saying a word. I tried the penis exercises the next morning. They didn't increase the size of my shaft. They did, however, cause the blood vessels on my mushroom tip to burst. It was weeks before I could fuck or piss right. Tanya didn't push the issue. Instead, she focused on getting me into a threesome. She knew she couldn't swing a dude so she tried to work the chick angle. She mentioned a few girls on our dance team. I didn't take the bait. She questioned my sexuality. I told her to get real. She asked why I was being so difficult. I told her I was a one-woman guy. She laughed like she might at her great-grandmother for mispronouncing some newfangled word.

"Are we living in medieval times?" she asked.

"No. But when I make a commitment to someone, that's it. I don't go sniffing around for other partners."

"That's not what I'm talking about. I'm talking about inviting someone we mutually agree upon and trust to enter our relationship and share our love. How can that be bad?"

"It's not bad. It's just not what I want."

"Oh, Lord. You know, most guys would kill to be in your situation."

"Well, I'm not most guys. I'm fine with threesomes when I'm single, but when I'm in a relationship, no dice."

She balled her fists and stormed off. I took the matter for dead.

A few weeks later, I was kicking it with Bert and Mason. We were eating Trader Joe's[212] orange chicken and watching TV. I got a call from Tanya. I could hear giggling in the background.

"What's up?" I asked.

"Oh nothing, lover. I'm at my place with Zulma, Amos, and Shoshi. They're visiting for the weekend and we're so bored. Can we come to your place and sit in the jacuzzi?"

"I guess."

"Yay. We'll be over soon."

They pulled up an hour later in Amos's red convertible. The windows were down, and I could hear them singing along to *The Grey Album*.[213] I stood on my walkway and waited. They parked on the street and got out. Amos was wearing khaki shorts and a pink tank top. His curly hair was in an afro and his face was unshaven. Zulma had on a Mario Bros T-shirt and orange capris. Her wavy black hair was around her shoulders. Shoshi was

---

[212] American grocery chain with over 530 stores nationwide. The first store was opened in 1967 by founder Joe Coulombe in Pasadena, California. While a typical grocery store may carry 50,000 items, Trader Joe's stocks about 4,000 items, 80% of which bear one of its brand names. Products include gourmet foods, organic foods, unusual frozen foods, imported foods, domestic and imported wine and beer, and "alternative" food items, such as vegan and vegetarian options. Many of the company's products are environmentally friendly.

[213] Mashup album released in 2004 by American musician, songwriter, and record producer Danger Mouse. It mixes an *a cappella* version of rapper Jay-Z's *The Black Album* with samples from the Beatles' self-titled ninth album, commonly known as *The White Album*. *The Grey Album* gained notoriety when EMI Records Ltd. attempted to halt its distribution despite approval from Jay-Z and Beatles member, Paul McCartney.

dressed in a white blouse and a miniskirt. Her short brown hair was streaked with red and shaved on one side. Tanya was in her standard purple sarong and black top. Her hair was down and her teeth were out. She bounced up and kissed me on the lips.

"Hey there, lover," she said.

I could smell alcohol on her breath. It made me want to drink. Amos took a case of pear cider from the trunk. I rolled my eyes and led everyone inside. I went to the kitchen and grabbed a bottle of vodka. I poured myself a tall, stiff one. We put on some music and drank. Things got sloppy. Tanya suggested we go in the jacuzzi. I asked her if they'd brought their suits. She threw her skinny arms in the air and cackled.

"We don't need suits, mofo. This is San Diego!"

"Actually, you do. It's a community spa and I could get busted if someone sees you guys in there naked."

"Oh, please. We'll take off our clothes and get right in the water. Nobody's gonna care."

She snatched my key and walked out the door. Her friends followed her laughing and singing. I looked at my homies.

"You got a real firecracker on your hands," Bert said.

"Don't I know it."

"Might wanna go and make sure they don't start snuckin'."[214]

"Good thinkin'."

I went into my room and put on my suit. I grabbed my towel and walked to the jacuzzi. Everyone was in the water naked. I snarled and banged on the gate. Tanya was in the middle of telling a story. Shoshi got out and let me in. I got a full view of her figure. She had a round ass and chubby legs. Her tits were small but perky. Her skin was peach and dusted with freckles. I fixed my shorts and thanked

---

[214] To have sex or intimate contact.

her. She smiled and flipped a lock of hair away from her face.

"No problem," she said.

I got in the water next to Tanya. Shoshi slid in next to me. My cock hardened. I focused on Tanya's story. She blabbed about how she and some other friends had done E one night in LA.

"It was so awesome. We took our shirts off and chewed bubble gum and did sexy poses for the camera."

Shoshi leaned over my crotch and grinned.

"I could be into that," she said.

"Haha, yeah," Tanya replied. "Sucks we don't have any ecstasy for tonight though."

"We can make our own kinda ecstasy," Shoshi said, looking up at me. "Right, Johann?"

Sweat clotted across my forehead.

"I guess."

The conversation dissipated. We got out, toweled off, and went back to my place. Zulma and Amos said they were tired. Tanya gave them her key and sent them on their way. She and Shoshi stayed behind and drank. They finished the pear cider and dipped into my vodka. This made them extra horny. Tanya sucked my neck and grabbed my cock while Shoshi rubbed her breasts and watched. Bert and Mason were in shock. They stared with their mouths open. I couldn't get into it with them gawking. I told the girls to go to my room. They ran off giggling.

"You better get in there and snit it,"[215] Bert said.

I smiled weakly. "Eeff,[216] man. This doesn't feel right."

Mason swigged his beer.

"If you don't grunge[217] in there, I'm gonna," he said.

---

[215] To have sex or intimate contact.

[216] I don't know; Who knows?; I'm sorry but . . .

[217] To go; to leave; to come; to spend (the night). (See Hans Joseph Fellmann, *Chuck Life's a Trip*, Russian Hill Press, 2019.)

His beard glinted with fire. I knew he was serious. I twisted my neck till it popped.

"Ait. Wish me luck."

I walked to my room and pushed open the door. The girls were on my bed in their undies. Tanya was on all fours miming a sex pose. Shoshi was squealing and clapping her hands. They saw me and got quiet. Tanya got off the bed and strutted to me. Her long arms and oval face made her look like an alien. She froze me with her gaze. Shoshi followed behind her. Her eyes were wide and hypnotic, and her boobies jiggled as she walked. The girls stopped on either side of me. They took my hands and led me to the bed. They laid me down and sandwiched me. They purred and cooed and rubbed my chest. The beast in my head grinned.

Fuck these bitches, he said. *Drill their asses. Cum on their faces.*

I was inclined to listen to him. Had I been single, I would have. I thought about my folks and their relationship: almost thirty years of monogamy and still going strong. I didn't wanna violate my commitment. I knew if I did, it would weaken me later. Not to mention, it would open the door for every other goddamned sexual act Tanya had been pining for. The whole thing was a no-fuckin-go.

I pushed the girls' hands off me and sat up. I heard Tanya groan.

"What's wrong now?" she asked.

"I'm not comfortable with this."

"Good Lord, what aren't you comfortable with? It's just Shoshi."

"I know. And if the circumstances were different, I'd be down. But we're in a relationship, Tanya. I can't do this."

"Yeah? Well, I can. Come 'ere, darlin'."

Tanya wrapped her skinny arm around Shoshi's waist

and pulled her in. They puckered their lips and kissed. The kiss turned into a smooch. The smooch turned into a long, protracted make-out. The girls hooked their legs together and fondled each other's breasts. I sat and watched. My cock jerked and gargled. My heart cracked and crumbled into dust. The girls stopped kissing. I stood and grabbed my pillow.

"Y'all have fun. I'm sleeping on the couch."

Shoshi got up and grabbed the pillow from me.

"Oh no you're not. Get in bed with Tanya. I'll take the couch."

She dressed and left the room. I clicked off the light and climbed under the cover. Tanya took a separate blanket and wrapped herself in it. We slept that way the night through.

Our relationship worsened. We still went to dance practice and fucked, but that was it. Tanya took more trips to LA alone. I spent more weekends getting drunk with my homeboys in front of the tube. Tim made frequent visits. It was almost like he'd moved in.

On a hot night in April, we were chillin' at our pad. I packed the hookah with mint tobacco and cracked some Fat Tires.[218] We sat on the couch and smoked and drank. Bert came charging through the front door. He had a big grin on his face and a dusty old box in his clutches.

"'S'all that bitchiness?" Mason asked.

Bert plopped the box down on the coffee table.

"Euro-trip videos from '85," he said. "My grandparents grunged over last weekend and blew me up with them."

Having nothing better to do, we stuck the videos in. We watched for hours as a bunch of old fucks puttered around the Bavarian countryside in a Fiat. I'm not sure how, but it got our trip juices flowing again. The prospect

---

[218] Amber Ale produced by New Belgium Brewing Company.

of a big one swelled in our collective mind like an engorged whale cunt. The timing was right for it. Bert and Tim were getting ready to graduate from San Diego State, as was I from UCSD. And Mason, who was also enrolled at UCSD, didn't give a fuck about finishing the last of his two years there. We agreed that in April '06, exactly one year later, we'd set off on the biggest trip any of us had ever done.

We cheers'd to make it official. We cracked more beers and drank and puffed away. I woke up on the couch ten hours later. My face was smashed into a pillow and my cheek was sticky with drool. I pried myself up and farted. I drank a slug of water and held my head. My phone buzzed on the coffee table. I grabbed it and squinted at its face. It was a number I didn't recognize. I wiped my eyes and cleared my throat.

"Hello?"

"Hmm, hello," said a man with a crackly voice. "Is this Johann?"

"Yeah, who is this?"

"This is Marshall. Tanya's father."

"Oh hey. What's up?"

"Well, our Pinto is in the shop. And Amos's car broke down."

"And?"

"Well, Great Gramma Guadeloupe needs her eight hundred milligram Advils. And we can only get those in Tijuana."

"So?"

"Soooo, it looks like we're gonna hafta take your car across the border to get them."

I nearly dropped the phone.

"Can't you give her four two-hundred milligram tablets?"

"Nope. She'll only take the eight-hundreds. Can you come and pick me up this afternoon?"

A forked road appeared in my mind. To the right, I saw

a life of travel, adventure, and blowing up, a trip around the world with my best friends, and year after year of writing material. To the left, I saw a life of fighting, infidelity, and misery, a trip to Tijuana with Marshall, and year after year of Tanya. My decision was clear.

"No can do," I said.

Marshall mumbled something. He said goodbye and hung up. A minute later, I got a call from Tanya. She apologized for her father's behavior but sympathized with his plight. I told her there was no way I was gonna pick him up in LA, take him to and from TJ, then drive back to SD, all in one day. She whined and said Danny woulda done it. I told her to call him. She scoffed and hung up. I went to my room and got on the Net. I started planning the big trip. I mapped out a rough itinerary: eighty-five days through Southeast Asia, India, and Europe. I stared at the world map on the screen. I felt a happiness I had never known. I resolved to put my blood into this one. I clicked off the computer and went to bed.

Tanya and I held on long enough to have our dance competition in mid-May. We broke up over the phone a week later. We met that day in the campus parking lot to exchange our stuff. Tanya looked melancholy. I gave her a basket of her things and she forced a smile. I forced one back. She handed me a bag of my crap and sighed.

"Can I call you sometime?" she asked.

"Sure."

I got in my car and drove away. The radio was playing "It Was a Good Day."[219] I went home and had one last cry. I

---

[219] Song by American rapper Ice Cube. It samples the Isley Brothers' "Footsteps in the Dark" and The Moments' "Sexy Mama," and was released on February 23, 1993, as the second single from the rapper's third solo album, *The Predator*. On the Billboard Hot 100, the song peaked at No. 15, making it his highest-charting single to date. Concerning the song's concept, Ice Cube stated, "The inspiration was

flushed my psyche of Tanya and her dirty poison. A few flecks of gold remained. I shoved them in a dark corner and went about my business. A week passed. I was on the toilet taking a shit. My phone buzzed on the counter. I picked it up.

"Hello?"

"Hiya, darlin'," Tanya said meekly.

"Hey."

I heard her signature sniffling. I steeled my heart.

"What's up?"

"Oh, nothing. I just miss you."

A turd fell from my anus and plunked the water.

"Johann?"

"Huh?"

"Don't you miss me?"

"Well—"

I heard Bert call me from the living room. We were in the middle of planning our trip. I yelled that I'd be there in a minute. Tanya started crying.

"It feels like you don't even wanna talk to me."

I tore off a sheet of toilet paper and wiped my ass.

"It's not that. I'm just kinda . . . ya know . . . busy."

"Busy? We've only been on the phone for a minute. We used to talk for hours when we were together."

"But we're not anymore."

"And that's another thing," she cried. "I was sure you'd come back to me before the week's end. Especially considering what today is."

"What's today?"

"May twenty-ninth, our anniversary."

---

my life at the time. It was the summer of '92, and I was in a hotel room, really in a state of euphoria . . . I was at the top of the rap game . . . I had all the money I had dreamed of . . . And I remember thinking . . . 'I rap all this gangsta stuff—what about all the good days I had?' . . . [So, I wrote] a fictional song. It's basically my interpretation of what a great day would be . . . It's a little of this and a little of that. I don't think you can pinpoint the day."

A spot of guilt burned my stomach. I zeroed in and snuffed it out. I stood and pulled up my pants. I turned and looked down.

"I gotta go."

I took the phone from my ear. I could hear Tanya sobbing on the other end. I clipped her silent with the press of a button. I shoved the phone in my pocket and flushed the toilet. My turds spiraled down and disappeared. I returned to the living room and joined my bros. We drank and smoked and planned grand adventures. It was only the beginning.